EINAR KÁRASON

STORM BIRDS

Translated from the Icelandic by
Quentin Bates

MACLEHOSE PRESS
QUERCUS · LONDON

First published in the Icelandic language as *Stormfuglar*
by Mál og menning in 2018

First published in Great Britain in 2020 by

MacLehose Press
An imprint of Quercus Publishing Ltd
Carmelite House
50 Victoria Embankment
London EC4Y 0DZ

An Hachette UK company

This book has been translated with a financial support from:

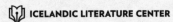 ICELANDIC LITERATURE CENTER

A CIP catalogue record for this book is available from the British Library.

ISBN (MMP) 978 0 85705 942 0
ISBN (Ebook) 978 0 85705 944 4

10 9 8 7 6 5 4 3 2 1

Designed and typeset in Scala by Libanus Press Ltd
Printed and bound in Great Britain by Clays Ltd, Elcograf S.p.A.

Papers used by Quercus Books are from well-managed forests and
other responsible sources.

With special thanks to Steinar J. Lúðvíksson

In February 1959, several Icelandic trawlers fishing in the Newfoundland waters were caught in exceptionally violent weather. The events that followed were the inspiration for this story, although the narrative and the characters portrayed are entirely fictional. Here, the trawler the story focuses on is called *Mávur*, which translates as the English word "Seagull".

At first glance, chipping ice off a ship seems to be a never-ending task. The ice not only looks like glass, it's as hard as glass, and when things are as they were on board our ship, then it's not just a thin, icy film which a child could shatter with a stone, more a vast crystal sculpture of waves and bulges, apparently moulded according to an artistic workman's notion of beauty, but in reality taking the shape of the ship's lines, primarily those of the hull. The big winches forward of the wheelhouse are suggested by large, convex lines, reminiscent of little mountains or ski slopes, while the deck's iron stanchions, for the fish pounds, might bring to mind the skyscrapers in America; the rails atop the gunwales have become a stone garden wall, the wires and stays, normally no thicker than a stolid bosun's thumb, have the bulk of sewer pipes, the trawl gallows on both sides have become mounds of ice, as has the superstructure and everything else on the boat deck, including what we would later rely on to save our lives: the lifeboats.

Then there's the raised bow, the whaleback with its winches and windlasses, all of it a bulging ice cap that could almost be the Vatnajökull glacier where the airliner *Geysir* crash-landed a few years ago, whose crew were found many days later, long after they had been written off as dead. The following spring, when they went to check on the aircraft and its cargo, it had been absorbed by the ice which grows thicker every year. The same happened to the plane fitted with skis that the U.S. Air Force sent up there to fetch the survivors, but which froze tight as soon as it landed and had to be abandoned as well. That one had also disappeared under the ice by the time soldiers arrived, only a few months later, to take a look at the accident site.

It was an endlessly thickening glacier such as this that the *Mávur*'s crew were now facing, every one of them wrapped in his warmest clothes, shod in thigh-high waders and with a waterproof oilskin smock over the top. Some carried hammers, others the deck spanners that are the trawlerman's universal wrench, some had lengths of pipe, meat mallets and heading knives, the bosun wielded the long knocking-out pin that ashore is called a crowbar, but the best equipped among them had the surprisingly modest ice axes, of which there were two on board. They went forward onto the deck, which was also sheeted in ice, so they had to hold on tight; normally this was easy enough when the ship rolled in heavy weather, but anything that could have provided a handhold had by now vanished under the layers of ice.

It was just as well that the roll had become much gentler than usual in this kind of heavy weather. The top weight of ice that had built up on it meant that the ship was less eager to right itself after rolling to one side or the other; although that didn't make things much easier, as it meant that the deck under their booted feet was never horizontal, it was always sloping. Then there were the breakers that surged in when you least expected them, deluging everything. That was when it was wise to hold on tight, because the cold sea had plenty of weight behind it, and these weren't mere splashes of water, but came in cascades.

Although the ice had the look of an ice cap or a crystal sculpture, it was easier to crack and break up than anyone would have expected. One decent whack on an iron stanchion, or where there was wire underneath, was enough to free a surprising amount, half a metre or more if it was a smart enough blow that hit the right spot. There's something satisfying about seeing the effect of your efforts, whatever work you're doing, and here it was right in front of your eyes. The crew put their backs into it, and after a few blows the rails that had been completely covered reappeared where they always had been. To begin with there was a certain enjoyment in all this, peering from under your sou'wester with water running down your face, watching the shards of ice shatter from a wire as broad as a barrel after a couple of swinging blows, seeing the pieces being scattered over the deck or out into the weather and the wind.

To begin with they made good progress, giving the ship back its proper shape. The working area reappeared, the colour of metal or painted brown, but mostly black. It wasn't hard to become absorbed in this work; although that was the one thing you shouldn't allow yourself to do, because you had to keep an eye out for breaking waves crashing over the deck and be ready to snatch at one of the newly uncovered handholds. The skipper was at the wheelhouse window above their heads, watching the seas around them, some of the waves so high that he had to crane his neck to see where they were headed. He had a knack for working out where they were going and would yell, "Breaker!" when one was about to crash into the ship. By the time the ship had shaken the water off, a new film of ice had already formed again on the iron surfaces that had been cleared and squared away just now. That thin covering thickened rapidly, swelled by more waves sweeping over the boat and by the spume that filled the air, blending with the swirling snow. It wasn't long before it was no longer just a film of ice, and there was nothing for it but to start all over again and break it off the same ladders and stanchions that they had worked so hard to clear just moments ago. By now their hands are a little more tired, and the clothes they pulled on before starting work aren't as dry and warm as they were; you build up a sweat under your smock doing this kind of heavy work, cold water finds its way down past your collar when you crouch to shelter from the worst of the seas, and there's always the chance that the water flooding the deck is going to be deep enough to fill your waders.

They made quick progress where they broke the ice on the wires, rails and casing, but that still left the ice caps covering the winches and the whaleback, which presented a greater challenge. They didn't tremble or sway when you landed a blow on them, but sat immobile, cold and silent like the glaciers of the wild highlands. The most powerful men with the heaviest tools set to work all the same, and were most successful when, as with the whaleback ladders, they broke away large chunks in one go. That presented a new problem, as these ice boulders began to slide and ground their way across the deck, and you did well to keep out of their way. Every seaman knows that the danger that comes from scraping against a lone drifting iceberg is greater than that of any other ice, and it was just such a berg that a few days before sank a new ship with almost a hundred people on board, in the same waters where *Mávur* had been fishing; and the same as the one that sank the magnificent *Titanic* with its two thousand passengers, half a century before – and these slabs sliding in the slush on the deck could easily injure a crewman. On top of all this, the ship had grown no lighter after the ice had been cleared from where it had collected, because the ice was still on board. Stray chunks like these had to be chased down with axes and clubs and broken down into pieces small enough to be washed out of the scuppers; the bigger pieces would have to be helped on their way and heaved over the gunwale.

Those first on deck to batter the ice worked with a rope tied around their waists and made fast to the ship. The men in the forward bunkroom had to stay there until a line had been strung from the casing to the whaleback, and only then was it worth running the risk of calling them up, to make their way aft as they held on to the rope. More men joined the crew on deck, and started to beat away some of the ice that had collected on the wheelhouse. They made progress, though a blow smashed a wheelhouse window right in front of the telegraph, where the skipper normally stood. Under normal circumstances, something would have been done right away to fix a cover over the open window, as the cold wind, snow and spray all made their way in. But the skipper immediately saw that it would be worth leaving this window open, at least for the moment, because the ice accumulating on the superstructure had largely obscured the others.

———

Four days earlier, they had finally reached the fishing grounds after the long voyage from Iceland, steaming for twelve hundred miles and passing south of Greenland's Cape Farewell on their way to the Newfoundland banks, where trawlers of various nationalities had been helping themselves to redfish for the last few years. As day broke on Tuesday, the third of February, the skipper gave the word for the trawls to be made ready, and the crew appeared on deck in weather that was still but cold. The temperature was minus five, despite the fact that they were a good way south of the latitudes they were used to on home grounds. But here the sea was cold, with the polar current flowing southwards between Greenland and Canada to meet the warmer current from the south; where they meet there aren't only heavy seas, but also plenty of fish preying on the feed that collects there, and plenty of life to be seen both in the water and in the air above. Overhead they saw a flock of kittiwakes making their daily morning journey to the northeast, the reason the Icelandic fishermen referred to this place as the Kittiwake Bank. There were other trawlers and crews on the same grounds: *Skerpla* and *Harpa* from Hafnarfjörður weren't far away, and they had been in touch with us over the radio; *Eyfirðingur* was somewhere to the north, along with the east-coast trawler *Garpur*, the newest and smartest ship in the fleet, sleek and magnificent, built in West Germany a couple of years earlier. They had taken a breaker, on passage somewhere south of Cape Farewell, and said over the radio that it had been like steaming straight into a stone wall. The starboard side of the wheelhouse had taken the full weight of the wave, which had smashed its seven windows as well as the deck lights, while the mate and those on watch found themselves waist-deep in water and the radio operator was lucky not to be washed overboard to port as the door was ripped from its hinges by the water flooding out. At first, they said to the others over the radio, it looked as if they would have to double back and return to Iceland, what with all the instruments out of action and the ship badly knocked about. But they managed to get pretty much everything fixed, and the first thing they heard once the radio was working again was the Mayday from the Danish ship off southern Greenland. They said they were sinking, so *Garpur*'s crew straight away set course along the bearing of the distress signal, but it took them too long to reach it. As they and other ships arrived at the position, there was nothing left, just some wreckage as far as they could see in the fog. An American aircraft circling above reported seeing a floating life ring. We on *Mávur* were expecting to be joined by the trawler *Poseidon* from Reykjavík out here on the Kittiwake Bank, and had reckoned on steaming in company with them all the way across, with both ships due to sail that same evening. But something delayed *Poseidon*, and they were kept back for a few days. That often happened.

Out on *Mávur*'s deck, once they had admired the kittiwakes, the men pulled on gloves and got to work, with each man's breath a cloud of vapour, and it wasn't just the air that was cold, the water at these latitudes was colder than anyone could have imagined. Most of us had learned at school that water freezes at zero degrees, so there had to be other forces at work here. It was because of the salt, said those who knew, and the sea itself here was two degrees below. It was as well to take care, not to be hasty and lose your footing, especially on the ladders up to the whaleback or the boat deck. A trawler from Iceland had lost a deckhand over the side earlier that winter, on just this same patch of ground, and even though the sea had been calm, the weather fine and they had been able to hook him back on board after only a minute or two, the cold had killed him stone dead. The man had begun to turn blue, was already going stiff, said one of the hands on board *Mávur*, and he knew what he was talking about, as he'd been on that trawler earlier that winter, when the deckhand lost his life.

Now for the trawls, two of them, rolled up and lashed to the gunwales on both sides, and now it made no difference if it was the starboard or the port trawl that was chosen to be shot away as everything was ready to go. No holes in the green netting; everything had been patched and fixed on the steam home from the last trip, and while we had been alongside in Reykjavík. The old man called out calmly from the wheelhouse.

"Get ready, starboard side."

On these ships the trawl warps were run through massive gallows, steel structures like an upside-down u, or an n the right way up, at both port and starboard gunwales, one on each side forward, close to the whaleback, and another aft by the companionway behind the superstructure, and when the trawl had been dropped into the sea and the warps had paid off the big winches in front of the wheelhouse, everything sang and howled while the crew on deck had little to do but wait, a couple of minutes with no work to be done. That was when proper seamen would reach one hand up under their smock tops and fumble all the way to the packet of Camels in their shirt pocket, shake out a white stick and catch it between their lips, light it with the flicker of a match shielded between palms, exhale a lungful of smoke, and turn over the cigarette to protect the glowing tip inside a cupped hand. There was a special skill to this that only the most experienced men had at their command, especially when the seas were heavy and squalls whipped the ship, and not least when the trawl was being hauled up, the wires emerging wet from the deep and the spray spitting out of the winch, where the warps groaned as they were reeled in. It's the job of the skipper or the mate on watch in the wheelhouse to steer so that the trawl is shot away just right and hits the seabed open. It's a giant bag with its mouth open so that it can snatch the fish on the seabed once everything's square and the trawler's at slow ahead, because with the fishing gear on the bottom the speed's kept low.

The bottom edge of the trawl's mouth has a jawline made up of what we call bobbins, steel balls that roll over the sea floor like the wheels of a jeep driving over every obstruction, protecting the belly, the underside of the trawl. Underneath the back end of the trawl, the codend, are fastened skins, cowhides, so that there's less chance of damage from spikes, rocks or anything else on the seabed. The top edge of the trawl mouth is strung with buoys or float-lines so that it stays open. Sometimes something would go wrong when the trawl was set, it would be twisted up so that when it reached the seabed the headline would be caught under the heavy bobbins, which would close up the mouth and there'd be no hope of anything other than a ripped trawl. Experienced seamen would sense that something wasn't right, they'd feel it in the ship's movement and when they put their hand on one of the warps, which shiver differently when the gear's hooked up, even though the warp from the ship down to the trawl could be a couple of hundred fathoms; and that was when there'd be nothing for it but to haul in again, check everything was square, and shoot it all back down.

Once the trawl has settled on the seabed, the trawl warps that lead back from each gallows have to be grappled together; once they're snatched into the same block the tension is balanced, and then the trawl doors, which are a little way in front of the trawl's mouth and each shackled to one of the warps, shear away from each other at an angle like two hands rising in supplication, palms facing, while the ship's progress and water resistance hold the trawl open, its mouth gaping in a gigantic grin, laughing at its prey. Once the trawl is on the seabed, a hook is sent running down the wire from a special winch on the boat deck to bring the warps together. When it has the warps in its grip and they have been drawn together at the ship's side, it's shackled into the snatch-block, the steel clamp by the companionway under the wheelhouse.

Then the trawl is towed until it's reckoned that there's enough fish in there, or as much as can be reasonably handled, and that's when the snatch-block is knocked open and the trawl hauled back up. *Mávur*'s skipper was as skilled as anyone in getting the trawl shot away square, in fact he was as skilled as anyone in anything to do with trawling, but even for these men something can go wrong; not that it happened often. This time, as soon as he had slowed down after shooting away for the first tow of the trip, he could feel that something wasn't quite right. He went out and checked the warps, touching them gently like a midwife checking on a poorly patient, and ordered the crew back on deck in their oilskins. No hanging around; even though half the crew had just sat down to steaming hot meatballs, cabbage, potatoes and melted butter in the mess, they all hurried out onto the deck.

First the warps had to be split, which as I said is knocking out the block. There's a heavy tool for just this job which is kept in the companionway under the wheelhouse, the knocking-out pin that's the size of a respectable crowbar. You have to stand well clear, as there's a fearsome tension in the warps when they're towing the trawl and its doors down there in the depths, and the power that's unleashed when they are freed from the block means it's as well not to be too close; all this calls for some strength in addition to the momentum provided by the weight of the knocking-out pin.

It was the bosun, on deck in his sweater and still chewing a mouthful of the meal he'd just sat down to, who hurried over to knock out the snatch-block. He was a powerful man, a tough character, afraid of nothing; he had been carried on board dead drunk and furious almost a week before, and it took three or four of the crew to manhandle that beefy body. He went out to the companionway in his sweater instead of oil-skins, picked up one of the spanners that are no longer than a man's forearm, and used that to knock out the warps, as quick as lightning. The block snapped open with a bang and the warps shot out of it, as tight as violin strings. The old man saw this and gave the bosun a dressing-down.

"I don't expect to see that kind of recklessness on my ship!"

The bosun muttered a few apologetic words, promised to

mend his ways and grinned to himself as he'd been sure the old man hadn't seen him; he refrained from retorting that everyone on board had seen the skipper himself go and knock out the block with a spanner when he'd decided that there was some urgency about getting the gear back on board. After a good while, the winches straining, the trawl came to the surface with the warps twisted around each other. That mess had to be untangled, and a rip in the headline, by the float-lines, had to be patched; it was quickly mended, so it wasn't worth switching over to the portside trawl. The "Shoot away!" call was repeated, and before long everything was square, and *Mávur*'s crew started picking up the Kittiwake Bank's valuable fish.

They were no more likely to see land than before. New-foundland was a hundred or so nautical miles away, that's close to two hundred kilometres, and they hardly came across another ship, even though the weather was clear and the visibility good. One or two trawlers could be made out at a fair distance, and a swarm of them out on the horizon; the second mate knew the seamen's handbook inside out as well as every ship in the Icelandic fleet, and as he was mending the trawl he said, after peering through the cloud of cigarette smoke around his face, that he reckoned those had to be some Russian factory tubs out there, sucking the seabed dry.

The skipper had by now kept the exhausted crew out in the foul weather since late in the day on Saturday, well into the night, and they had made progress on the ice that could be seen on the fore part of the ship, so he decided to give those who had been on their feet the longest a rest. One by one they made their way aft, pulled off their smock tops and waders in the oilskin store, went to the mess for the coffee, sandwiches and more that the cooks had prepared for them, and then smoked for a while, in silence; there wasn't much to be said, because everyone could feel that the trawler's motion was nothing like what they were used to. It rose and dropped into the troughs, but rolled much more slowly than it should, considering the state of the sea and the wind, lingering for a long time at the end of each roll. For a long moment it heeled frighteningly far to port, and after having finally righted itself it rolled to starboard and declined to come back. The whining of the pumps could be heard, as the engineers transferred fuel from the tanks on one side of the vessel to the other, from port to starboard and back again. The main engine was idling gently, and it was reassuring to hear its rumble, because if the big diesel engine down below failed their end would not be far away. After a while they went to the free bunks aft, most of them lying down fully dressed so that they'd be ready, and the lucky ones fell asleep right away while the others listened to the wailing weather and the hammering of the ice clubs wielded by those who continued the battle out in the darkness.

The skipper was in the wheelhouse, and he had a feeling that the weather was beginning to calm down. Storms like this often pass through in the space of a dozen hours, and this one had been raging for twenty. He hoped that the crew's efforts in chopping away the ice were showing results. More than ten men were still out there in the heavy weather, and there weren't enough tools for more than that. They needed better tools, and he knew that it had been a mistake to set sail for these distant grounds in the middle of winter without enough ice axes for the whole crew, but who could have expected extreme conditions like these? The radio operator was with his equipment, in the radio room that was at the aft side of the wheelhouse, from where calls and a hiss of interference could be heard, and he came out to the skipper and the deckhand at the wheel to tell them that there had been a Mayday call from a Spanish trawler on the same grounds, but still a good distance away, and a Canadian trawler had reported itself in difficulties from heavy icing. He had gone on to make contact with the *Harpa*, which said that it was making progress, but that they were struggling with heavy icing and a list as they tried to ride out the storm. The other Hafnarfjörður trawler, the *Skerpla*, was on its way home, having set off the day before with its fishroom full.

We on board *Mávur* also tried to manoeuvre, and with the wind being north–north-easterly the only thing for it was to head into it, let the waves roll over the bow and keep the propeller turning at low revs, as a wave catching the ship broadside or astern would be enough to sink or at least capsize it. They judged that there was no possibility of responding to the Spaniard's distress call. The old man stood at the telegraph, issuing occasional orders for the propeller to be clutched out, disengaged, and when necessary going astern when a heavy wave appeared out of the blackness. He knew that the whole engine room crew was on duty, ready to respond quickly, and they were doing just that. All the same, the skipper called for the chief, wanting to know how things were down there. He came up to the wheelhouse and reported that as things stood everything was fine, but he was concerned that a heavy list could drain the oil and stop the engine, but the engine was reliable and ticking over as it was supposed to, all thirteen hundred horsepower of it. They were constantly pumping fuel between the port and starboard tanks, but weren't able to do the same with the freshwater tanks as these had all frozen, apart from a small one which the heat from the engine was keeping liquid, and which would serve for their cooking, coffee and drinking water as long as the crew didn't get too thirsty. They discussed how the engine room crew could make some clubs using whatever they had available, and the chief said he'd do what he could, maybe cut lengths of pipe and weld bolts and pieces of metal to them, to give them weight. The skipper told him not to make them too heavy, because even if each blow from the big axes and sledgehammers was effective, those kinds of tools rapidly tired out the crew.

When the chief had gone below again, a vast wave appeared, towering high above the masthead lights. The skipper yelled out of the window to the crew on deck to grab hold of something, just before it crashed over the ship. The ship listed to port and lay there for a while; although the water that had cascaded over it drained away, it didn't right itself. He called out to the men to get themselves inside if they could and not risk staying on deck with the ship listing so heavily, and when the first mate came up to the wheelhouse the skipper sent him below to wake all those who were in their bunks, because now everyone would need to be in a state of readiness, whoever they happened to be. That is, if it wasn't already too late. They could feel the ship shifting slightly, heeling further to port. They looked at each other; they knew that it wouldn't take a big wave to capsize it now, and that would be the end of them.

The skipper added that the mate should tell the crew that it'd been two hours since the last shift was called off the deck to get some rest, and from now on the rule would be two hours' rest a day until the worst of it was behind them. They heard the pumps whine as the engine room crew tried to shift weight to starboard, and eventually they could feel the ship gradually right itself.

The mate hurried below, telling the bosun to call all the hands, most of whom were already awake, but when the mate came to where the second mate lay, there was no sign of life. The mate called him again, but got no reply, and he shook him in his bunk, terrified that he'd suffered a heart attack; but the man replied in a clear voice:

"I think it's best if I lie here while the ship goes down. I've been a seaman for years, and I've never seen anything like this. This is death itself."

"In God's name, get to your feet, there's no point thinking that way," the mate said, and hurried back up to the wheel-house.

The second engineer was there; he and the skipper had been out on deck and had seen that the portside lifeboat was iced over, and almost full of water, no doubt mostly frozen. It would be no use to them, whatever happened, and it was pulling the already listing ship over even further because in that state it weighed several tons. Getting rid of it was their best hope. Freeing the lifeboat was a task that called for men with experience, strength and nerve; the deck was sheeted with ice and offered few handholds, which would make things danger-ous once the huge weight was free of its fastenings, as it could take on a life of its own and then nobody would want to be standing too close.

Then the second mate, who not long before had refused

to leave his bunk, appeared in the wheelhouse with a darkness in his eyes, and after listening to the discussion about the lifeboat, he spoke up.

"What are we waiting for?" he said, and added that he was ready to go and slip the lifeboat. Two deckhands volunteered to join him. "It's up to you," he said, to the first who stepped forward.

The youngest deckhand on board, eighteen-year-old Lárus, offered to help, but the second mate decided that it would be unnecessary and unwise.

"I reckon it's enough to lose three men if things go wrong," he said.

The skipper did everything he could to keep the ship head to wind and as steady as possible while they were at work around the boat, and the three carefully made their way out, knocking ice off the rails and anything else that could provide them with a handhold. They reached the lifeboat and hammered the ice from the fastenings. Then they hacked at the cradle straps and falls with axes, and as these gave way the lifeboat slipped from its cradle into the sea, alongside the ship. They could see in the glow of the ship's lights that it was floating upright, but hardly any of it was visible above the water's surface. Then it drifted away aft and was lost in the gloom. The ship immediately righted itself smartly, and the youngest crewman, Lárus, was relieved, even though it was strange to watch it disappear into the wide ocean, this craft that should have been their last resort if things took a turn for the worse.

————

When Lárus joined the ship on the thirtieth of January, more than a week earlier, he was consumed by both excitement and anticipation, although his mother, who had gone with him together with his father, was fearful, saying that she had a feeling of dread and her dreams had foretold something bad. His parents had driven him in the family's Willys jeep, and there was a touch of pride about his father at the wheel, because his son was off on his third trip as a trawlerman and had already been spoken of as the kind of grafter who didn't shy away from work. That was what his father had heard from the dock workers, who heard all the dockside tales. The young man's last trip had been on another trawler, which hadn't been such a decent berth as this, and like this present trip that, too, had been to distant waters, all the way up to the Barents Sea in the far north, inside the polar circle.

"We're almost at the North Pole!" one of his shipmates had said, and as it was midwinter, there hadn't been a glimpse of sunlight the whole time. It'd been black night round the clock, broken only by a sight of the moon or stars when the clouds parted, or when the Northern Lights danced in the sky. But that hadn't happened often and never lasted long, as most of the time the weather was foggy, the seas rough and the fishing poor, so that a deckhand's share was small. But now *Mávur* was heading for Newfoundland's fishing grounds, and Lárus had heard some fantastic stories of those trips, with long steaming-times to and from the grounds, separated by a short, sharp spell of fishing with unbelievable catches, heavy fishing for redfish that sold for high prices both in Britain and in Germany. There was even a chance of a run ashore overseas, with all the fun that would come with it, and a fat envelope at the end of everything. Because his mother was poorly, and his younger brother too, there was no denying that his parents would be both happy and relieved if he could bring home his share of a successful trip.

The trawler lay there at the quayside, with *"Mávur* RE-335" painted on the bow. They got out of the car and he pointed out to his mother how sturdy and magnificent the ship was, a real floating fortress, more than seven hundred tonnes of steel. The bow was a fine sight, with its raised whaleback, which seamen generally just refer to as "up for'ard", and then there was the deck, the area where the crew worked while fishing, where the catch was dropped onto the deck, and there were the hatches to the fishroom. The superstructure with its towering wheelhouse and forward-facing windows was amidships, behind it was the lower structure containing the mess and accommodation, and above that there was the boat deck, where the two large, solid lifeboats hung in sturdy steel gallows known as davits, one on each side.

Lárus' father had plenty of sea time in the herring fleet behind him, and from where they stood by the Willys, admiring the ship, he was able to appreciate that this trawler, like all of the new vessels in the fleet, had particularly impressive lifeboats which, given the opportunity, could even be used to fish herring, when they would deploy a seine around a shoal of herring.

"They even have engines!" his father said, with pride in his voice.

Anything connected to seafaring and the sea fascinated him. A Sunday drive with the family would frequently take them around the harbour, so that they could take a close look at the ships and boats – where this one had come from, what kind of fishing that one had been doing. When other seamen were around they would discuss things down to the finest detail, and a couple of weeks ago the family had stood with a throng of townsfolk, practically in the same spot, as they were given the chance to look over the Danish fleet's latest flagship, the specially built Greenland cargo liner *Hans Hedtoft*, brand spanking new and off on its first voyage to Greenland. This was a two-thousand-two-hundred-tonne ship specially strengthened for the waters in the far north, and an absolute gem of a ship for both passengers and cargo, a ship finally able to serve Greenland's settlements all year round. There were even guns on board.

"As well to be prepared for anything!" Lárus' father had said.

It was from here, two weeks before, that *Hans Hedtoft* had set course for the most southerly point of Greenland, the same course that *Mávur*'s crew would be setting later that evening, after the family had admiringly looked it over. The sailing at eight had been announced on the radio after the midday news bulletin. The sound of an engine came from *Mávur*, the rapid buzz and diesel chatter of a generator; ice had been stowed in the fishroom, every fuel and water tank had been filled, stores had been put on board, whole carcasses, sacks of potatoes, a barrel of salted meat, coffee, bread, ham, bottles of milk, porridge oats, rice, sides of pork . . . the lights blazed, more men turned up, some of them drunk and noisy, each with a kitbag in his left hand and a bottle swinging from the more reliable right.

Lárus glanced at his mother, knowing that she would not take well to seeing drunk men making their way to the ship that would be her son's lifeboat and home in those cold and distant waters for the next few weeks. She had woken that morning with a strong feeling of foreboding and had tried to dissuade the boy from sailing on this trip, but he'd already agreed to go, and the last thing he wanted to do was earn himself a reputation for unreliability and failing to keep his word; his father said that these western Newfoundland fishing grounds were known for their placidity and mild weather, and on top of that the fishing would be so good that it would take the trawler no more than a few days to fill up and then they'd be on their way home.

Despite her feeling of foreboding, father and son had persuaded Lárus' mother to step out of the car, and they admired the robust diesel-powered ship that would take the lad to distant waters, so she said no more, but kissed the boy and wrapped her arms around him, asking God and good luck to accompany him; she didn't say another word about those disturbing premonitions, as it would have been wrong to predict disaster on the eve of a long voyage. She knew a few things about seamanship and the dangers of the deep. His mother had never been a seafarer, but had lost her own father to the ocean, as well as her brother and grandfather. Seafaring from Iceland could be as dangerous as soldiering in times of war.

———

Once we'd arrived at the Kittiwake Bank off Newfoundland, a week's steaming from Iceland behind us, the fishing was nothing special to begin with. The trawl was fouled in that first tow, as I've already said, and after it'd been shot back it came up again torn to shreds, as if it had burst from being overfilled after only fifteen minutes in the water. We switched trawls and shot the portside one away, while the netmen on board set to work mending the ripped gear. Deckhand Lárus was put to work on the needle basket, winding twine around the broad netting needles; the mending crew's quick hands meant that they soon needed to be reloaded. Lárus wound both mending twine and seizing twine onto the needles, and watched the menders with admiration as they worked with bare hands to fix the trawl, which was heavy with water, wondering how they knew what was what. These were men who only a few days before had been dead drunk, insensible, with bloodshot and bleary eyes, their faces traced with broken blood vessels; but now they knew at a glance how many meshes were needed here and how many knots there, and where nothing more than a crow's foot needed mending.

Down below, the bunk where Lárus slept had clearly not too long ago been occupied by a net mender, as someone had taped a massive diagram of a trawl net to the deckhead, with everything marked, the wings, bellies and codend, each marked with a figure for the number of pickups or meshes. Lárus was determined to absorb as much as he could of all this, so that one day he could become a time-served net mender, one of those magicians capable of dealing with the impenetrable heap of netting piled on the deck, soaked through and covered in scales. As an experienced mender, he'd be able to start anywhere and see right away precisely what was what, even in the dark, on a rolling deck, in heavy weather and with sleet coming down. He'd see how many knots were needed here and there, and then he'd pick up a knife to cut away the half-empty needle, dropping the netting on the deck.

"Job done," he'd say.

This kind of slack fishing tried everyone's patience, with many strong words flying about on the deck. They cursed the trawl, the sea and the chill in the air, even though the temperature wasn't much more than four or five degrees below, only a little colder than the sea – or maybe big words and curses helped them stay a little warmer. But up in the wheelhouse, where the skipper or the mate stood watch with the deckhand at the wheel, it was warm, and they didn't curse, merely giving instructions or pointing with a stern look: haul, give way, let go, switch over.

Then things started to look better; you might say that the fishing was fabulous. Tows lasted just ten or twelve minutes, and when the codend approached the surface it would shoot out as if pumped full of air – which in fact it was. The scarlet fish, once released from the crushing weight of the pressure far below, would puff up and their pink swim bladders would expand and stick out of their mouths, beyond their jaws, as if the fish were blowing up balloons or bubbles of Bazooka gum.

As everyone knows, redfish are bright red, not the light grey, blue or murky yellow that's good enough for other fish, and redfish are also dangerous, armed with particularly sharp and hard dorsal spines that go straight through rubber gloves or even thick boots; on the other hand, redfish don't need that much handling. There was no gutting and stripping out the offal, instead they went down to the fishroom whole. The fish were gaffed out of the pond where they'd been washed, and dropped into baskets which were then emptied into the fishroom, onto a chute leading straight into the pounds. Part of the crew was down there to take delivery of the fish and pack them into pounds, where they had to be mixed with the right measure of ice, the ice that was dumped down there before they sailed. It was lying there in a heap, partly fused into a hard pile which a deckhand broke up with a pick, while others scooped ice into the pounds and then shovelled a layer of it over everything, again and again. Pound boards were hooked into the stanchions one at a time to close the pounds as they filled up, and eventually it became an effort to shovel fish into them, as the pile rose above head height; but there was no use complaining – although there was nothing wrong with cursing the lousy redfish if you were stabbed by a bone, each curse accompanied by clouds of breath in the cold air.

When fishing was slow, or even just average, the fishroom hands would go below to ice over the last haul, and the work would be finished while the trawl was still in the water. This gave the men an opportunity to pull off smock tops and boots and sit in the warm messroom, have a smoke and a mug of coffee, let their thoughts wander, spout an opinion on the state of the world or listen to their shipmates' mutterings; but there was none of that now. It wasn't long before the trawl was full to bursting again and hauled up from the sea bed, while the men stood on deck as the winch whined, dripped and even spat water, quickly snaked a hand under their smocks to pluck a filterless cigarette from a breast pocket, lit up a match even though the box was damp, and crowded around the one who had the light sheltered between his palms.

The catch was brought aboard one lift at a time. Taking the full weight of the codend over the deck in one go was out of the question: trying it would have been enough to capsize the boat, and it couldn't be done anyhow, because the ship didn't have the power for it, or a wire strong enough to take that kind of tension. The fish in the aftmost part of the trawl, the codend, were brought up with a rope known as a strop looped around it and hooked to the gilson, a lifting wire which hangs from a boom long enough to swing far out to the side and back over the deck. The end of the bag was tied with a knot that looked like those used to hang condemned men at the gallows, the kind they have in westerns, except that this knot could be freed with a sharp pull; and that's what the bagman did, as he fumbled beneath the codend wearing his smock and sou'wester, as water and guts streamed from it, jumping quickly aside as soon as he'd slipped the knot and the catch flooded over the deck. When the fishing was like this there would often be fish stacked high against the gunwales, if some of the previous haul's catch hadn't got as far as the fishroom yet.

Every hand was needed on deck when the fishing was this heavy, and as much of the catch as possible needed to be stowed below before the trawl was hauled up again – something that didn't always work out – and the fishroom crew worked up a sweat to keep up with the flow of fish coming from the deck above. So they stooped, shovelled and hacked, some of them stripped down to their shirt sleeves, even though it was cold down there.

On these trawlers, the shifts were such that the crew worked six hours on deck and had six in their bunks, and so on; half the crew were on duty at night and in the afternoon, while the other half worked the morning and evening shifts. But when the fishing was heavy, as it was now, shift work was suspended and the most you would get would be six hours out of every twenty-four to eat, wash and rest, and nobody complained. Old guys who had worked coastal boats trotted out the old saying: Staying awake for a spring season's no hardship.

"I can sleep when I'm dead," others said.

Of course, everyone knew that with the shifts suspended and the fishing this heavy, the ship would fill quickly, and there would be plenty of time to rest on the week-long steam home.

That's the way it was. On Tuesday everything was either foul, smashed or a lash-up, on Wednesday it all came together and the crew put their backs into getting the fish below, which is how it continued through the night, the following day and then another night, and by then it was Friday, the sixth of February and the fishing was no less heavy, while the weather remained calm and so did the sea. Visibility was good and they could recognise other trawlers. Somewhere out there was *Harpa*, and *Poseidon* had reported that it was there along with *Garpur* and the West Germans, British, Canadians and Russians, all of them shovelling up the scarlet redfish with their spines that stabbed your finger, causing sores that became infected. During Friday, *Mávur*'s skipper saw that the trip was coming to an end and the fishroom would be full sometime that night. At daybreak on Saturday he let it be known that they wouldn't be fishing much longer; all that was left to be done was to get the rest of the fish down below and square the ship away, and soon they would be steaming home.

The skipper was in the wheelhouse on the morning of the seventh of February, the day the storm hit, and he realised that they mustn't lose any time filling up and getting the ship ready for steaming, as all the signs were there. The Canadian weather service had issued a storm warning for the Kittiwake Bank and its surroundings, and winter storms in these waters could mean wild seas. There were other signs as well, that there was something in the air: no sign of the usual morning flock of kittiwakes over the area, though their arrival was something that could normally be relied on; a swell that was gaining weight, a sure sign that heavy weather was to be expected, although there was scarcely a ripple to be seen on the water around *Mávur*, which had begun ponderously rising and dipping with the swell with the four hundred tonnes stowed away in its fishroom; day should have broken by now, but it was still strangely dark, with the gloomy sky the colour of lead, even though there was little by way of cloud cover overhead; the barometer was dropping like a stone, and when the needle had fallen alarmingly far the skipper tapped its glass there on the deckhead, whereupon it fell a little further and pointed straight at the word "Storm".

But the deck was full of fish, which the whole deck crew was hurrying to stow away as fast as possible, as there wouldn't be a moment's rest until the job was done. Both trawls were on deck, and the doors still swinging over the side in their gallows. Men were instructed to get them inboard, chocked and shackled in place, but tying the trawl down in the usual way was going to take too long. The bosun and a couple of hands set to work to tie the trawls and secure them with chains under the whaleback. The wires were spooled onto the winch drums and shackled; if there was going to be bad weather then it would be as well not to have to worry about a wire that could come loose and foul the rudder or the propeller.

———

When the young deckhand Lárus had said farewell to his parents and waved as the Willys drove away, he went up *Mávur*'s gangplank. He went to the wheelhouse and reported to the first mate who was there, who told him that the crew were beginning to turn up and everything was almost ready, so he should go and find himself a berth in the deck crew's quarters, forward under the whaleback; he could then get himself a cup of coffee from the galley. Lárus carried his kitbag across the deck, opened an iron door and then another one beyond it, and made his way down a couple of steps. There were two cabins, and from both came loud voices, drunken talk and clouds of tobacco smoke, and Lárus wondered whether he dared go in there. There were a few more steps leading further down, so he followed them to another cabin with bunks either side of the door and nobody about. Well-travelled kitbags lay in two or three bunks, and a blanket in another, so Lárus found himself an empty one in the top tier and shifted some of the junk to make room for his belongings. Loud, slurred voices could be heard from above, along with the squealing of the ship's plates against the tyres used for fenders when in port.

He went aft to the galley, where he met the mess boy, who was a lad of his own age. They told each other their names, and Lárus accepted a mug of coffee and a slice of solid bread spread with cheese. Then the mate he'd spoken to in the wheelhouse put his head around the door, and said to Lárus that the last of the men was being brought on board and they'd be sailing right away, and told him to go up to the whaleback and help with the mooring ropes. After that he could go and get some rest, but should be ready to take a steaming watch.

"You're sober, aren't you?"

The sound of the engine rose to a roar, and Lárus nodded to the mate and made his way up to the whaleback to join another of the crew, and together they watched as two men struggled to get a third on board, a broad-shouldered, powerful man, dead drunk and angry, who was swiping at the pair and telling them that this shitpot of a ship could go straight to hell, and they could go with it. The mate joined them; between them they managed to support the big man up the gangplank, and disappeared with him forward under the whaleback. Lárus didn't get a good look at the man's face, but was sure that he recognised him from somewhere. They heard the drunk muscleman start roaring with laughter, and then the steel door clanged shut and the sound was muffled.

The moorings were lifted from the bollards on the quayside while Lárus and his companion hauled the ropes on board; the trawler inched astern and the propeller whipped the surface into a foam at the ship's side, and the bow crept away from the quay until the stern ropes were thrown off and *Mávur* swung around to head for the harbour gaps, the lights winking at either side of the entrance. The lights and buoys in the sound blinked at them as they steamed past a cargo ship and a couple of trawlers, the sea of city lights slipped away behind, and so began the long trip to the Newfoundland fishing grounds off North America.

When Lárus went below to the lower cabin it was no longer empty, and there, in one of the bunks, lay the bear of a man whom it had been such a struggle to get aboard. He recognised the man right away: he had been bosun on the trip he'd been on before Christmas, on another trawler, all the way up in the darkness of the far north.

He crept into his bunk and lay there while the ship's movement became more pronounced the further behind they left the harbour and dry land, the bow lifting and plunging. The rumbling of the diesel engine aft made its way to every corner of the ship and its vibrations reached through walls, decks, and the planks of the bunks, while from above came loud voices and the clinking of bottles, along with snores and discontented mutterings from the other bunk. This was what Lárus fell asleep to. He had no idea how long he had slept when a loud clank woke him, accompanied by the feeling that he was flying. The smell down here was the stink of dirty mattresses and unwashed clothes mingled with the smell of fish, plus old tar and tobacco smoke, all of which hurt both his nose and his throat, and he was dizzy. Lárus felt cold, though he was sweating under the thick blanket. He didn't normally suffer badly from the sea; but now the pitching was deeper, and then he was hoisted as if he was in a lift shooting upwards, and then the ground pulled away from under his feet – or, rather, his back – and he and the ship were in a free fall which ended in the rushing noise of the sea, and again there was that deafening clank, as if the bow right next to his head had collided with something hard.

There was no change in the ship's motion: it continued to rise and fall, and the deepest plunges resulted in that terrible metal bang, as if someone had smashed the ship's cheek with a giant sledgehammer, maybe Thor's hammer itself, right against the bow and next to Lárus' ear. He thought things over, and was convinced that there had to be something badly wrong; whatever it was had to be serious, and soon there would be calls and shouts and activity, with everyone ordered up on deck, since there was every chance that the boat was in real difficulties and about to sink. All the same, there were no unexpected shouts to be heard, other than from the tipsy voices in the cabin above – but what would they know? They were all too drunk to take an interest in anything as trivial as the trawler sinking beneath them. The same went for the snoring bull in the other bunk. Now the bow rose high in the air, and in the same movement was thrown over to port where the young man lay, and he could feel the ship drop back into the water, and then the dull clank was repeated, louder than ever. In his fright, Lárus jumped to his feet, fumbled for his shoes, pulled on a sweater and trousers, and climbed to the top of the steps, where he hauled open the steel door and peered out.

Most of the wheelhouse windows were dark except for a mere glimmer of light, but the sidelights lit up the ship's wake by each gunwale; water was gushing over the deck as the trawler pushed its way through the waves. Lárus relaxed, closed the steel door behind him and made his way across the deck, along the companionway under the bridge wing, and then went inside and up to the wheelhouse. The mate was shrouded in a cloud of pipe smoke, and the deckhand at the wheel had a half-smoked cigarette between his lips. They both looked up as Lárus came in, but neither of them in an unfriendly way, so perhaps it was a change to have someone appear in the darkness of the wheelhouse. Lárus knew they were both waiting for him to speak, to give some explanation for his presence. He tried to appear calm and asked how far they had covered, but his voice sounded reedy and afraid. The mate asked if he was feeling poorly or if he was having trouble sleeping, while the hand at the wheel looked at him sympathetically and puffed smoke in his direction. Lárus coughed and explained that he was fine, but there was so much noise up forward where he had been sleeping, as if they were always hitting buoys or something. The mate glanced at the man at the wheel and grinned, saying that he hoped they hadn't finished off all the buoys on their course. He added that they were punching the tide off Reykjanes, and, given the heavy swell, every time the boat pitched the port anchor would shift a little and slam against the plates. It had been like that for a long time.

Lárus tried to make out that he hadn't been in the least anxious, but asked if it could be fixed, hoping to sound unconcerned. The mate's reply was that undoubtedly it could, but the question was whether or not it would ever be done, as the owners weren't in the habit of responding very quickly when the crew complained over a little discomfort. He said that over on *Eyfirðingur* from up north the crew had complained that the trawler was a wet ship, and it was even known as "the Swamp", because it frequently dipped its bow deep into the waves. But nothing was done until a few years later, when the trawler was on the slipway and someone happened to notice that the forward fuel tank was full, and had been since the ship was built. Everyone had assumed it was empty, but there'd been more than a hundred tonnes in there, pulling her down by the bow.

"*Mávur* can be pretty damned wet as well," said the man at the wheel. "Has anyone checked if there's some mysterious extra tank forward?"

"No," the mate said, adding that he was sure nobody had. "This one doesn't lie as low at the bow as *Eyfirðingur* did."

The man at the wheel was the oldest of the deck crew, almost seventy years old, and later on in the trip Lárus asked him why he hadn't quit this seagoing slavery.

"I can't do anything else," the old man replied.

Then the mate told Lárus that he'd be called in the morning for a turn at the wheel, and with that the boy made his way forward, happy to be running over to the whaleback again now that the water wasn't sweeping over the deck. When he was back in his bunk in the lower cabin there was yet another clank from the anchor, but he felt reassured, knowing that the world wasn't coming to an end. And the bosun's bulky figure was still there, still snoring.

During that last trip, on the other trawler, deep in the Arctic blackness, there had been a problem with a leaking cap on one of the tanks. It was supposed to be completely sealed and was screwed down tight, but perhaps it had cross-threaded, because water was frothing both into and out of it. Lárus wasn't sure if it was a freshwater tank or a fuel tank. The engineers had been trying to tighten up the cap, and finally brought out a long-handled pipe wrench which three deckhands put their weight behind, trying their hardest to tighten the cap, and they managed to shift it slightly. They checked, but it still wasn't fully tightened. Then the bosun picked up a spanner, placed it around the cap and gave it half a turn with one hand, and that did the trick.

———

What the bosun had looked forward to after a trip in the darkness somewhere up near the Arctic circle, apart from simply having solid ground under his feet, was to be reunited with the woman he lived with, and her daughter; they had been living together for about a year, which meant that they spent the days that he wasn't at sea together. His absences were always long ones, because in those days Iceland's fishing grounds were crowded with British and German trawlers, as some nations found it hard to accept Iceland's expansion of the fishery limits off its coast, as demonstrated during the Cod Wars. Britain had sent warships to protect its trawler fleet against the smaller craft that Iceland called its Coast Guard, which the British referred to as "gunboats", and while this was going on the Icelandic trawlers sought out more distant fishing grounds, such as the Barents Sea, the waters around Jan Mayen and Svalbard, off Greenland, and as far as the fertile redfish grounds off Newfoundland.

When the trawlermen finally stepped ashore after many weeks at sea, they had the experience of a harsh existence behind them, with shifts that kept them working for twelve hours out of every twenty-four, meals in the mess in-between, maybe time to have a wash or comb their hair or perhaps to open a book, but otherwise it was revolving rounds of sleep and work, no fun and not a drop of anything alcoholic to drink. So what do fishermen do, when they're finally ashore? They do pretty much the same as people there do at weekends while trawlermen are fishing: they dress in their best, in polished shoes, a white shirt and a bootlace tie, and drop in to Röðull or the Breiðfirðingabúð, and there will certainly be a trip to the liquor store for a drop of something heart-warming, as the trawlers never docked at weekends. It was always a Monday or a Tuesday, those most everyday of all everyday days, when normal people go to work. That's when the fishermen get into taxis half-cut and unsteady on their feet, as happens when you're no longer in the habit of drinking, have been riding the waves for weeks on end and are ready to make up for all those bone-dry weeks of toil, which was how the bosun felt whenever he stepped ashore. First he'd enjoy his homecoming, wrap his arms around his wife, see the brightness shine in the child's eyes, and then there would be a lull, until he arrived home in a taxi, his white shirt smeared with grime, the bootlace tie askew, a half-empty bottle in one hand and his best shoes with their nylon soles scored with damp grit in the other; and by then the joy of homecoming would have ebbed away.

But now, finally ashore for a Christmas break after that long and unpleasant Arctic trip, five weeks for not much more than the minimum daily rate, he was naturally excited by the prospect of coming home to a warm, clean bed with his wife between a white duvet and sheets, having the chance to sleep the whole night through, chatter with the youngster and spend time with people he was fond of. But bosuns don't just jump ashore along with the ropes: there are things that need to be put in order on board first, and by the time it's finally alright to head for the quayside and look around for a taxi, some of the crew already have bottles in their hands. One of the deckhands on his shift has been up to the dockside café and ordered a decent taxi that turns up right away, as well as two bottles of akvavit that are standing there on the table, and of course they call out to the bosun himself, that tower of strength, seafaring hero and bear of a man, as he arrives to collect his kitbag.

"Can't we offer you a dram to drive out the chill?"

And there certainly was a chill, along with all that Arctic

darkness that had filtered through his senses and deep into his soul, so how could he deny himself a drop of good cheer? It wasn't as if it would do any harm. But time passed, and before anyone knew what had happened they were in the basement of the People's Palace and it wasn't until the next day that the bosun was able to collect enough of his wits to get a taxi home, by which time he'd gone from sleepiness to wakefulness, and had a few more drams to help him summon the courage to make such a big decision. That was the final straw for the woman he lived with, and she announced that there was no sense in having a man she only saw every few weeks, and then only dead drunk, and within a quarter of an hour she had packed her clothes and the child's and departed in another taxi, while the bosun was left to sit and come to the conclusion that he was a man and could take this kind of fuss, and that he wasn't going to be upset by some woman's hysterics. All the same, he was upset enough to decide to wade out into the sea and end it all, and he managed to fulfil the first part of his intention – wading deep into the water near the Fossvogur filling station – but he didn't end it all because, while nothing had changed about his opinion that life was worthless, he discovered that the sea itself was vile, his own workplace was both cold and filthy, and he couldn't bear the thought of filling his lungs with this muck, shivering out his life in the cold. It would be better to sort this out on dry land, wearing warm clothes and maybe among company, so instead he went to look up some old friends, determined to drink himself to death with them, and hopefully to spend his last moments drunk and laughing.

He had been working steadily towards this target for more than a month, and felt that as he'd been coughing up blood for a good few days he had to be making good progress, but he hadn't completed his self-imposed task yet when, in a moment of weakness, he let himself be persuaded to join *Mávur* for a trip. That's why he'd raged so furiously when he was hustled or carried on board, since it would screw up those plans.

———

The next morning Lárus was at the wheel, standing there in a jersey, thick trousers and waterproof shoes. It was seven o'clock and still pitch-dark, the way it is this far north at the end of January, and they were out on the open sea, course set for the southern tip of Greenland, and there were no landmarks to be seen here, no lights and no shipping in sight. The weather was gloomy, with rain hammering against the wheelhouse windows, and the wind and current were against them so that the bow sometimes pitched deep into the waves to send a spray of water up and over the whaleback and crashing against the wheelhouse. The navigation lights on the ship's sides glowed, but in the wheelhouse it was dark except for the glimmer from the instruments, radar and compass that Lárus had been told to steer by. He kept the lubber line pointing south-west, and stood there at the wheel trying to keep it steady, while waves and currents shoved the bow away from the correct course by a few degrees, requiring a little rudder the other way to right the ship's head, but not so much that it would swing back too far. From his experience as a trawler-man, short though it was, Lárus knew that a steersman, the one who stood at the large wooden wheel which the older hands referred to as the helm, took a professional pride in making these movements as slight as possible, and Lárus did his very best, smarting with self-reproach whenever he over-corrected and went from port far over to starboard. But that didn't happen often, and he was doing a good job. At any rate, the mate didn't complain – and neither did the skipper, who soon appeared in the wheelhouse with a mug of coffee to relieve the mate.

The officers exchanged a few quiet words about the weather, the course. The skipper nodded to Lárus, who didn't feel that it was right not to introduce himself, and the skipper nodded again.

"That's fine, lad," he said, and disappeared into the chart room at the back of the wheelhouse, where the radio and the bank of communication equipment were, leaving Lárus alone in the wheelhouse to stay on course. There was nothing but an endless seascape all around, and now it started to brighten up over a world that was all grey and white: the waves, the spume and the sky, as well as the occasional storm bird gliding past. Lárus thought he saw a black-backed gull following the ship – his own namesake; in a book of Iceland's birds that he had been given one Christmas, he'd read that the bird's name was *Larus fuscus*, and all the gull family were *Larus* something-or-other.

The crew could be seen out and about, appearing under the whaleback and making their cautious way aft to the galley and mess. Lárus had tried to have a cup of coffee before his turn at the wheel, coffee with milk and sugar like he was used to at home, but had hardly taken a sip of it before the nausea he'd been suffering from in his bunk as he listened to the anchor's hammering against the hull welled up again inside him, and he'd emptied his mug into the sink. The nausea disappeared as soon as he took his place at the wheel and stood there shifting his weight from one leg to the other as the ship rolled.

A man who turned out to be the radio operator appeared; he introduced himself to Lárus, said good morning to the skipper, who replied in a low voice, and sat down at the bank of equipment. Interference and voices could be heard on the radio, and the Sparks answered, announcing *Mávur*'s call sign and exchanging a few words; then he came back into the wheelhouse and told the skipper that he'd been in touch with *Harpa* and *Garpur*, both of which were not far ahead of them, maybe half a day or so, and he'd heard that *Poseidon* had been delayed and was still at the quayside.

It was light in the wheelhouse now, so Lárus was able to see what it looked like; it seemed to him surprisingly clean and smart, with green matting on the floor and walls panelled in dark wood, and the instruments, door handles and the metal surrounds of the windows were polished and gleaming. The wheelhouse had a faint smell of oil about it, and a faint aroma of fish blended with tobacco smoke. The skipper stood at the wheelhouse's starboard window, the one fitted with a circular wiper which swept off the rain and spray so that you could always see through it. The skipper also had the telegraph to hand, labelled in English – full, half, slow, dead slow, stop, astern – which he could use to ring the required speed through to the engine room crew. He also had a copper pipe that led to the engine room, which could carry his voice down to the engineers and allowed him to hear what they had to say.

The skipper was a middle-aged man with dark hair that was turning grey, a man of average height who said little and replied in a quiet voice when anyone spoke to him, when the radio operator or the mate came to give him some piece of information – except when he needed to call down to the engine room or to the deck, when his voice was stern and powerful. As Lárus would find out during this trip, the skipper could make himself heard when necessary, such as when he had to hand down instructions to those working on deck; then his voice carried clearly over the whining of the winches and the howling of the weather. Lárus would later hear one of the other deckhands remark that their skipper's voice was so loud and powerful, that when there were many trawlers fishing in home waters – such as the Hali grounds, where they often fish in a tight group – and the old man yelled out of the window to shoot away, twenty other trawlers would immediately shoot their trawls away too.

———

Once the portside lifeboat had vanished into the ocean, *Mávur* returned to an even keel, hardly rolling, as if buckling under the weight of the ice. The skipper stood by the telegraph and the speaking tube, at the shattered window, watching the waves that kept lifting the ship and then dropping it into troughs, and the old man's experienced eye told him that the waves were fifteen, twenty metres high. It was vital to stay head to wind and weather; *Mávur* was such a sloppy ship in a following sea that with all the ice, not least the glacier that enveloped the whaleback, the anchor windlass and the rails, any seas breaking astern would plunge the bow deep into these giant waves. On the other hand, it felt strange to keep this course and inch deeper and deeper into these cold seas. But that didn't bear thinking about. The skipper knew that sooner or later he would have no choice but to send a party to start on the hazardous work of clearing some of the ice from the whaleback, but for the moment this was still far too dangerous. They would have to wait for conditions to improve, as these heavy seas were continuing to wash over the whaleback, where there was no handhold, nothing but ice.

He also had to rely on the engine not developing any problems, which it rarely did, this solid, reliable, English-made powerhouse, but it was being pushed hard now, from full ahead to slow, stop to astern, and that's when something's liable to give. There were men out there on the wheelhouse roof, hacking at the superstructure, and he could hear the blows and rumbling up there, where everything was frozen solid, even the radar. The scanner had stopped turning and there was no way of knowing if other ships were close by. The *Harpa* was no longer answering; Mayday calls had been heard from two or three foreign ships, but it was difficult to make them out on the radio, as there was so much interference.

Some of the crew were also up on the lower superstructure aft of the wheelhouse, which we call the casing. Like everyone else, they'd been given strict instructions to always remain roped to something solid on board. All the same, the skipper was uneasy about having them out there. Every ship's officer's nightmare was that something would happen to any of the crew. There was always a pleasure to hear an old skipper with a lifetime, whole decades, in the wheelhouse behind him say that he hadn't had a crewman lose so much as a little finger.

But now he had other things on his mind, as a twisting knot of a wave tumbled towards the ship, a little to port and about as big as all seven floors of the *Morgunblaðið* newspaper's newly completed building in Reykjavík. He managed to haul the door open and yell "Breaker!" to the men beating ice aft on the casing, and slowed the engine just as the wave broke over the ship. It was thrown to the side, heavy in the water, as the wave hurled its full weight at the superstructure and gushed in through the open window. *Mávur* lay so far over to starboard that the men in the wheelhouse had to hold on, and the wave flooded over them as the ship heeled further and further and refused to right itself.

Soaked to the skin, the skipper opened the door and ordered the crew on the casing inside, and they trooped in, one, two, three, four, until they were all there, wet through and cold, but alive. The skipper rang the telegraph back to call for half speed ahead; he feared that, with such heavy list, the propeller would break the surface and the rudder with it, and that would be the end of *Mávur* and every man on board. He yelled into the speaking tube, but the engine room was clearly on the alert already, because the engine picked up and they could hear the pumps whine as the fuel was shifted over to the portside tanks.

The men who had been aft were all obviously in shock. Three of them sat slumped like children on the wheelhouse floor, staring at the floor or gazing in front of them with blank eyes. Several more climbed the alarmingly angled steps into the wheelhouse, fear on their faces. Those who had cut the portside lifeboat adrift earlier in the day were there as well, and now the second mate asked if it was time to let the starboard boat go too.

The skipper was far from happy that so many of the crew now knew that desperate measures were needed, that if the ship were to sink there would be no saving them; and it was as if the second mate could read his thoughts.

"Aren't there a few rubber boats on board?" he asked.

On the skipper's orders, he and two others went aft to the boat deck armed with axes, and tied themselves to the rail. The silent and pale crew heard blows and hammering, and then a great weight dropped over the side and the trawler began to right itself; ponderously, perhaps, but it was enough. The engine was still running, the rudder still responding, and every splash of water froze when it met steel.

Those on board knew that the sea was below freezing, that they were caught in the cold polar current, and that they would have to find their way south into warmer waters. But in order to do that they'd have to come about, turn the stern to the wind and run southwards before the weather, which as things stood didn't bear thinking about any more than any other option. They hadn't been able to keep up with clearing of the ice, and it was building up again. The big winches were lost beneath a mountain of ice that reached up to the wheelhouse windows, and then there was the glacier up there on the whaleback. The ship's motion had improved after the lifeboats were cut away, but now it quickly began to worsen once more. As many of the crew as could armed themselves with axes, spanners and lengths of pipe, in the hope that they'd be able to keep pace with the spray, the cold and the ice, praying to God that the weather wouldn't get worse, but improve.

It was Sunday, the eighth of February, and almost midday. Now the smell of food came wafting from the galley, which was somehow cheering, like the aroma of good food always is, even that of the condemned's last meal, but what would we know about that? The old man pointed at half the men in the wheelhouse and told them to get out on deck and work on the ice. He told the rest – the ones who'd been caught under the big wave as it crashed onto the casing and nearly drowned them all – to go below and get some hot food inside them, and then to go out and relieve the others. Then he called down the speaking tube for the chief engineer and asked him to come up. He wanted his advice on what could be done about the glacier that had formed over the trawl winches, and whether or not it would be possible for the winches to be run for a moment, in the hope that this would crack the ice from them.

The chief engineer was a young man, just into his twenties, but all the same the senior man in the engine room. There were five of them looking after the engine, three engineers and two greasers. In this kind of weather there were always two on watch, so that they could react quickly to instructions from the wheelhouse or to anything that might go wrong down below, while the others were either smashing ice on deck, trying to snatch some rest or else sawing lengths of pipe for makeshift ice clubs. The chief had learned his trade on just such an engine as this, a 1322h.p. Ruston, while the older engineers were more accustomed to the steam engines that the fleet had run on for so long.

Down in the engine room, in the heat and the furious noise, it was somehow to put out of mind the dangers facing them; not put them out of mind entirely, but ignore them just enough to allow you to focus completely on the engine, the heart of the ship, and ensure that it continued to beat, and forget that the weather outside was like a war zone somewhere in foreign parts. When any of them went above and up to the wheelhouse to see for themselves how things were, there was nothing for it but to bite the bullet and accept it.

The week-long voyage to the fishing grounds had been mostly quiet. The ship had ploughed along its course, the officers reckoning by compass and the distance steamed, working from the log, the torpedo towed on a cable that turned a wheel on the gunwale at a speed that varied depending on how well the ship made way, and taking into account margins of error, a position could be reckoned at the end of each steaming watch. Lárus was told to take a turn at the wheel a few times, which he enjoyed and considered a great responsibility; he stood on watch with the mates and sometimes with the skipper, and there would be visitors from the engine room, or the cook, or sometimes deckhands wanting to know what progress had been made, and the radio operator – a man who knew so much – was generally there as well. He also looked after the ship's books in their two boxes, forty in each, from Reykjavík's lending library for ships; boxes that found their way from one ship to another, and which were refreshed a couple of times a year so that the crews didn't have the same reading matter all the time.

There was little that needed to be done on the long steam. Of course the officers on watch were in the wheelhouse, while the cooks managed the meals and the clearing-up, and the engineers ensured that the engines ran smoothly and were properly lubricated, and fixed anything that needed to be fixed. But the deckhands could take it easy, and at first many of them were dazed or hungover, but on the second day they were already on their feet. The netmen and those with experience set to work on the fishing gear. It was usual to overhaul the trawls while steaming off, checking that they weren't worn or damaged, but *Mávur*'s trawls had already been overhauled before this trip and were ready to be used, so they remained where they'd been stowed. But the crew went over the wires, the sweeplines and the bang-bang ropes, splicing something that needed it or where a splice would do no harm, and some of them enjoyed the work; though this was a complicated business which called for both skill and strength, as the individual wire strands were teased apart with a heavy steel spike and then twisted together with others, according to seamanlike rules. Hands were also set to work to clean the ship and rub down the interior, swab decks, buff copper, polish the wheelhouse panelling and bring every metal surface to a shine. The mate told the crew to look after the cleaning of their own quarters, both aft and in the fo'c'sle, with variable results, and in the lower cabin forward, where Lárus and the bosun had made themselves comfortable, there didn't seem to be much to be done. That bear of a man, the bosun, was quiet to begin with, keeping to his bunk and not showing his face much, sometimes sitting up for a smoke, or to turn the pages of a book. If his and Lárus' paths crossed and they both happened to be awake, he'd say a few friendly words to acknowledge the lad he remembered from that Arctic trip. On the third day the bosun was on his feet, and from then on he appeared in the mess at mealtimes and made himself at home there. He'd borrowed a couple of books from the collection the radio operator kept in his shack, and lay on a bench in the mess, smoking one cigarette after another, a mug of coffee at his elbow as he read. Lárus came in, meaning to treat himself to a coffee and a smoke, but the sweet, milky coffee still brought back the nausea from when they'd beaten their way through the weather as the ship steamed off; although he wasn't seasick, and his appetite was fine. It was a shame about the coffee, just as it was about the cigarettes he was trying to smoke, the whole carton of filter cigarettes he had bought for the trip, until he found that drinking his coffee black and snapping the filters off the cigarettes made the sour taste and nausea vanish. That was a wonderful discovery, and Lárus felt that he was a better seaman for it. As he sat in the mess wearing a checked flannel shirt, with a cigarette and a mug of black coffee, and reckoned that this was going to be his life's work, he tried to make out what book the bosun was reading. He made out from the cover that it was "*Wayfarers* by Knut Hamsun".

"Is that a good book?"

It was a moment before the bosun realised that the question was meant for him; he eventually looked up from the book and at Lárus, before glancing at the book's cover to check the title, as he hadn't bothered to before.

"It's about travellers who don't have a home anywhere," he said. "That's the sort of people I know."

Later that day, Lárus went up to see the radio operator and asked if he could take a look at the library. The Sparks always welcomed anyone on this kind of errand and was happy to offer his guidance, and the general opinion on board was that he'd read pretty much every book in the fleet's book chests. And now the youngest deckhand was here.

"What are you looking for? Something decent, maybe? There's poetry, Davíð Stefánsson and Steinn Steinarr. Did you know that our bosun once published a book of verse? Oddur Björnsson's publishing house in Akureyri published it. *Lines from the Darkness*, I think it's called, or maybe it was *Lines from the Twilight*, but unfortunately we don't have it on board."

Lárus left the radio shack with a seafaring book, *Breaking Waves*, tales of disasters and adventures at sea, published by Iðunn in Reykjavík in 1949. Books like this one were his father's favourite reading matter, and their house in the Bústaðir district had a row of them lined up on the living-room shelf, although Lárus didn't recall having seen this one. The Christmas just gone, a brand-new one that had been advertised in the papers had appeared at home, *Across the Hungry Sea: True Accounts of Heroism, Disasters and Adventure* published by Ægir in 1958. Father and son had devoured the book, which had given them plenty to discuss: the last voyage of the *El Dorado*, the tragedy of the *Andrea Doria* and the sinking of the *Lusitania*, as well as a long and dreadful account entitled "I Survived", by someone who had done just that during the worst maritime disaster known, when the giant *Wilhelm Gustloff* was sunk in the Baltic at the end of the war, packed with refugees from East Prussia fleeing the advancing Russians. There were eight thousand people on board, and fewer than a thousand were saved as the rest vanished into the ocean. It wasn't easy to believe it, but six times more people lost their lives in this disaster than had disappeared into the deep with the *Titanic*. All the same, there seemed to be no other maritime disaster that equalled the loss of the *Titanic* on its maiden voyage in 1912. Lárus had read illustrated accounts in newspapers and magazines, the kind of reading material that his father wasn't fond of; instead he had a thick book, either Danish or Norwegian, all about this disaster from half a century ago. The two of them had often looked through it, ever since he was a child, examining the map which showed the assumed location of the sinking, and the pictures of people rowing away from the sinking ship out there in the open sea.

So Lárus sat in the mess alongside the bosun and poet, with this ten-year-old book called *Breaking Waves* which he had borrowed from the Sparks, with stories of disasters in

Icelandic waters, and immersed himself in an account of a trawler caught in the lethal storm that struck the Hali fishing grounds on the eighth of February 1925, almost thirty-four years ago, this being the first of February. The descriptions were hair-raising.

As the bosun put aside his book about travelling people, Lárus told him what he'd been reading about the ice building up on the trawler in the storm on the Hali grounds as nearby trawlers capsized, and asked the bosun if there was a chance that they could experience that kind of weather.

The bosun lit a cigarette.

"We'll be a good way further south," he said. "The Hali grounds are north of the Westfjords up by the Arctic circle, and I gather the Kittiwake Bank we're heading for is on around the same latitude as London. But who knows? Anything can happen, although in my experience it's always been calm there."

That same day the news came through that the new Greenland cargo liner *Hans Hedtoft* was in difficulties, as the crew broadcast that they were sinking off the southern point of Greenland, now far from *Mávur*'s position, on the same shipping route. That magnificent ship that Lárus had admired in port in Reykjavík a couple of weeks ago had called in at Greenland, picked up passengers and cargo and set off for Denmark, when something had gone dramatically wrong.

"Mayday, Mayday. We are sinking."

Word filtered down to *Mávur*'s crew that the skipper and the mates had gone over the possibility of changing course to head for the position the distress call had come from, and worked out that it was too far away. The *Hans Hedtoft* had already sunk, they'd never be able to make it in time, and there were other ships already on their way, including the trawler *Garpur* which had sailed from Iceland ahead of them and had a better turn of speed. The news came through later that nothing had been found, apart from one of the *Hans Hedtoft*'s life rings, leaving the fifty passengers and crew given up for dead.

Lárus continued to turn the pages of his book of maritime disasters whenever he had time to read, and its accounts became all the more horrific because he knew that they had been so close to just such a tragedy.

The mess was often busy with card games in the evenings, and sometimes they played poker for matches or cigarettes. Some of the crew lounged around reading the various contents of the radio operator's book chests – biographies, war stories; one of the engineers was reading Laxness, Iceland's Nobel Prize winner, and would occasionally shake with silent laughter. Someone asked what was so funny, and the fellow from the engine room replied by reading out the entire passage recounting Jón Hreggviðsson's adventure in Rotterdam to the mess – the lanterns hanging over doorways, and how he was approached by a lady who was so well dressed that he was sure she had to be the wife of a priest or a dean of the church, who spoke so kindly to him and asked him inside to be entertained. She found the silver coin in his purse and her welcome was no less warm for that, so he slept in her rooms that night; but during the night two vagabonds came and threw him out, "and with that Jón Hreggviðssoń's silver coin had vanished".

There was a gale of laughter as the reading came to a close.

"I used to go to Rotterdam when I was on the freighters, and I reckon I've met this priest's wife," one of them said.

Lárus, the youngest hand on board, enjoyed his lookout shifts, and had already made it known that he was willing to take turns at the wheel. A man could stand there, in tune with the ship's movements, looking out into the darkness or the daylight, out over that huge, endless but changing ocean. Bright daylight would come with the arrival of the low sun mirrored in the blue surface, and then the mate would go out onto the bridge wing with a sextant to sight the sun as the radio gave its time signal, and from that he could calculate their precise position to mark on the charts back there in the chart room. The dead reckoning position that they'd already worked out was not far off, but their heading had to be corrected, as they were further north and east than they'd intended, so the course to be steered was altered by a couple of degrees southwards.

The previous summer, on one of Lárus' first watches at sea on a trawler, they had been towing in sunshine and fine weather south of the Westman Islands, not far off Súlnasker, when one of the crew pointed seawards, not far from the ship's side, where a pod of orcas, those magnificent black-and-white whales, were swimming and breaching, in circles after circles. They were so close that their breathing could be heard.

"They've found feed," said one of the deckhands. "More than likely they've cornered a shoal of herring or capelin."

The news travelled fast, and before long there were guillemots circling over the cauldron the orcas had created by swimming round and round. Then the guillemots began to dive, nose first like fighter planes, one after the other, vanishing with lightning speed below the surface, sometimes many of them at once, before bobbing back up with regal expressions on their faces, hard eyes, and each one with something in its beak. The humble grey gulls lost all interest in the trawler and any guts that might be dropped over its side, and instead went to take a closer look at the spectacle taking place among the orcas and the plunging guillemots.

From there, Lárus gazed northwards to the Westman Islands that sat in the dazzle on the sea; a fleet of boats could be seen nearby, and beyond it the black sands, green pastures and icy peaks, and that was when Lárus decided that he would be a seaman his whole life long. And now here he was, at the wheel passing Cape Farewell, the southernmost point of cold, vast Greenland.

Up in *Mávur*'s wheelhouse, where Lárus stood at the wheel keeping the course set south-west, the radio operator, a man constantly with his nose in a book, began to talk of how our forefathers had sailed this same route from Iceland, passing the tip of Greenland before following the west coast in their open wooden ships; much smaller than a steel trawler like this one, maybe twenty-five metres in length or less, at most half the size of *Mávur*, and of course with no engine, just a sail, and no deck.

Both Lárus at the wheel and the mate puffing his pipe at the wheelhouse window found this an unnerving thought, and the mate asked if it wasn't true that half those ships sailing to Greenland had sunk or been wrecked, because he was sure he'd heard something to that effect.

"Yes, some of them sank or vanished," the Sparks agreed. "But as we well know, that still happens to ships today."

He added that back then they would sail only at the height of summer, and certainly not through any winter storms, although naturally any kind of weather could just as easily be encountered in summer.

"But how did they find their way?" Lárus asked. "It's impossible to understand. They didn't have radar or a compass or a sextant. How the hell did they do it?"

The radio operator replied that these ancient seafarers *could* have had some kind of sextant, something to measure the sun's height above the horizon, and it was likely that they were able to read the stars, navigating by the Pole Star and such like.

The mate laughed, as he had not long ago taken a sight of the sun.

"You need to know what time it is, and I don't suppose they had clocks – or a time signal over the radio or from a coast station!"

"Well, hold on," the wise radio operator said. "There's one precise time they always knew, as long as they could see the sun, and that's the sun at its highest point. At any rate," he added, "they crossed the open ocean back and forth, from Europe to the Faroes, Iceland and Greenland, and always found the right place, home to their own fjord, their own bay, even all the way to America."

"That hasn't been proved," the mate said.

But the radio operator was adamant that there was no reason to doubt it, since America and the sailing route to it had been described in old books, and they had probably crossed the Kittiwake Bank itself.

"Think of it! A thousand years ago!"

Now the second mate came into the wheelhouse, and the chief mate brought the conversation to an end.

"Well, those fellows didn't have a galley and cooks on board like we do, at least. I'm going below for a bite to eat!"

———

It was late on Sunday and the storm had raged for more than a day and a night, and the radio operator quietly told the skipper that he had been trying to make contact with *Harpa*, but there was no response. The reason he'd been trying to contact them was that earlier in the morning he thought he'd heard – he wasn't sure, but he was becoming increasingly certain that he had, the more he thought it over – an indistinct distress call from *Harpa*, saying that they were going down, and then nothing but interference, nothing more. He hadn't been able to make out the whole of the call sign, or it had been transmitted too late, but the "Tango Foxtrot" part meant that it was an Icelandic ship.

The skipper went pale as he listened, and they were both aware that they were in much the same situation that *Harpa* had been in, not far away on the same fishing grounds. *Harpa* was a similar ship to *Mávur*, and had also filled its fishroom on Saturday morning, fully loaded and lying low in the water, just like *Mávur*. It now looked likely that three ships had been lost since the storm began to rage a day ago, and it was clear that the next one to sink would probably be

Mávur. They knew that *Eyfirðingur* was some way to the south, in warmer water, and it would be best for *Mávur* if they could make their way there as well, which would be an eight- or ten-hour run under normal conditions; but conditions now were far from normal, and to get there they would have to turn and run before the weather, which could be lethal.

Since they'd cut away the lifeboats, lightening the ship, it had handled better for a while, but now it was again becoming ponderous, again listing under the weight of the waves without righting itself, without swinging back like a pendulum, and it had become a matter of life and death to be rid of the glacier of ice that had formed on the winches forward of the wheelhouse, and from the whaleback over which the waves broke constantly. It went without saying that anyone going up there would be taking his life in his hands, but they had no choice.

The radio operator suggested that they should broadcast to other ships and shore stations that they were in difficulties, icing heavily, but the skipper's view was that it wasn't advisable, or even worthwhile. Every crew out here on these waters had enough problems of its own; that's to say, those the storm and the crashing waves hadn't already sent to the bottom.

"Let's wait a while. We'll see."

———

The crew was already tired when the storm broke over them on Saturday, the seventh of February, after the heavy fishing of the preceding days, when everyone had been on deck day and night to deal with the redfish and get the catch into the fishroom. Since then, few of them had had an opportunity to rest, because the skipper had ordered that everyone should get only two hours out of every twenty-four until all this was behind them. Now it was late in the day on the eighth, and the frost was no less harsh than it had been, and neither were the storm or the spray. Mountainous waves rose, fell and broke all around the ship. The crew naturally needed nourishment to give them the strength they needed to fight for their lives, and the head cook decided that the best of everything would give them the most energy. Carcasses stored in the ship's cool room were brought out to be chopped up and cooked; roasted in the oven and fried in pans, as many as the galley stoves could cope with, and he made sure that the meat was on the messroom tables in bowls, so that the men could eat quickly with their fingers, and save time. There were bowls of steaming potatoes, boiled in their skins, and a constant flow of flasks of fresh coffee. The crew came off the deck stiff from the cold, still in full oilskins, to grab a piece of leg, a chunk of roast or chops that they gnawed on as they held them in their fists, helped themselves to a few hot potatoes, and knocked back a mug of coffee before returning into the foul weather, the spray and the cold.

The crew also needed to relieve themselves; what with the cold and the battering the heads down below no longer worked, but there was one toilet up in the wheelhouse that was still functioning, and that's where everyone went, to the little cubbyhole right up against the smokestack, and they had to be careful not to touch the hot tinplate around the exhaust with their bare backsides. But it was certainly warm in there.

The wheelhouse was told that there was plenty of hot food to be had around the clock below, and they dashed down for a bite; except for the skipper, who didn't leave his place at the telegraph by the open window, where he had coffee, cigarettes and a tub of snuff. The cook brought up a roasted shoulder joint which the skipper could help himself to without having to take his eyes off what was unfolding before him.

There's no denying that the crew were fearful, although they tried to forget it while they were out in the cold, hacking at the ice. But it came rushing over them again as they went inside to sit down or take a nap. The first to break down was a deckhand, who shook so uncontrollably in the messroom that he almost passed out, and when he tried to stand up he turned out to be so weak at the knees that he fell flat on the floor, and there was nothing for it but to help him to a bunk. There were no tears, but one man sitting in the mess suddenly began to laugh, and he laughed and laughed, burst into a fit of coughing, and then continued to howl with laughter, so that it hurt to hear him, leaving those around him feeling helpless. Those who broke down in tears could be comforted, or at least encouraged to toughen up, but what can you do with someone who just laughs? It wasn't an infectious laugh, and nobody joined in. At last – and it was just as well – the man's laughter came to an end, and he pulled on his hat and sou'wester again and went up above to crack ice off the superstructure, with a slightly shamefaced look.

The bosun also felt that death was close at hand, and was afraid of it, which was remarkable, because only a few weeks ago there had been nothing he'd wanted more than to be dead, and had even started working towards that end. He remembered that he had backed out of swimming out into the sea as the thought of salt water snuffing out his life was more than he could bear, so now that very thing was staring him in the face, and there was no other prospect than an unpleasant death in salt water – but at least there was a reason to keep fighting against it. The bosun's weapon against the ice was a sledgehammer, which was effective but so heavy that anyone who wielded it would be able to feel it in his entire body afterwards; but that was no reason to slow down, they just had to bite the bullet and ignore the pain if the ice-cold sea wasn't to claim them all. Young Lárus chose to stay close to the bosun, as that way he knew he was in the right place and doing the right thing. The bosun was the strongest man on board and the hardest worker, and by following his lead Lárus wanted to show that he, too, was a grafter, or so he hoped. He followed the bosun when he went inside to eat, and they left their oil-skin smocks by the door and sat down, gnawing at freshly roasted meat and potatoes, washed down with glasses of milk and mugs of coffee, and the bosun could see that the youngster was trembling, even though the lad was holding his glass of milk in both hands to hide it.

"You've got the horrors?" the bosun asked.

A lump suddenly appeared in Lárus' throat. It happens like that, when people become unexpectedly aware of someone else's concern, and he had to swallow, shake it off, and managed to say, was forced to admit, that maybe it would be best to lie down and go to sleep, to sleep off the impending death.

"You'd wake up," the bosun said with a humourless grin. "The cold water'll come flooding in, and then it won't be good to be shut in. If I were a rat, I wouldn't want to drown in my hole."

———

Lárus went up to the wheelhouse to use the toilet. The bosun followed him up to talk things over with the officers, and both the skipper and second mate were there. They agreed that some of the crew would have to go up onto the whaleback to try and dislodge some of the glacier that had formed there. The ship's movements had become very slow, righting itself with alarming sluggishness as the waves shifted it back and forth. Water would come over the gunwales and slop against the superstructure before the ship could pull itself clear of the cold water again. Just as Lárus came back out of the toilet, the second mate and the bosun had decided that they would both go forward, and needed a pair of reliable men to take with them. He immediately volunteered. The second mate was about to protest, as he felt the lad was too young and inexperienced.

"I can trust this one," the bosun said.

The four of them set off for the ice-covered bow. It was daylight, but the skipper nevertheless switched on the deck lights that were still working. There were still waves breaking over the bow and flooding the deck, and the skipper maintained a slow speed through the seas while the lookouts in the wheelhouse watched for approaching waves, so that they could warn the men forward to hold on tight as these passed over them. First they had to smash ice off the steps leading up to the whaleback, breaking large slices and chunks that then needed to be contained and held in place while they were broken into smaller pieces which could wash out of the freeing ports.

They worked their way up onto the whaleback itself, where

they could scarcely get a hand- or foothold. They tried to keep themselves secure, holding on to anything that had been cleared of ice with one hand and hacking at the ice with the other. Lárus and the other deckhand had axes, the bosun and the second mate each had a hammer. Now they were up on the ice cap itself, the whaleback, and there hadn't been a breaker yet, just a few splashes of spray, and now they needed to work fast. They could see the results right away, as they took off a lump of ice with every blow, and little by little the ship's painted steel could be made out under the steel-hard ice. The four of them hammered as hard as they could, and by the time they felt they'd got rid of most of the danger that threatened to drag them all nose-first into the depths, they were absorbed in their task. Although the skipper's foghorn of a voice was reputed to be powerful enough to reach a whole fleet, the steel echoed under the beating they gave it, and by the time they heard the lookouts' warning of the wave that was about to break over them and engulf them like an avalanche it was too late.

The second mate was hurled backwards off the whaleback, down onto the deck, where he landed on a stanchion before being pinned up against it. The bosun and the other deckhand managed to grab handholds, but Lárus, who was furthest from the bow, snatched at thin air as he was caught up in the deluge of ice-cold water that dragged him along. In a second or two he would be somewhere out there in the tormented sea. He felt something grab at him and catch him by the collar. His collar tightened around his neck, and for a moment the young man thought that either he would choke to death, or the smock would give way, and the rushing water was so powerful that everything around him cracked and groaned. Things remained that way for an eerily long time, as nature with all its might pulled the young man one way, towards the sea, while a single fist held him back.

"And I weigh more than eighty kilos . . ."

Finally the wave passed, and everyone was still on board. Figures appeared aft on the deck, to help the four men. Three of them immediately said that they were fine – although Lárus coughed so hard that probably nobody understood what he was saying – but the second mate was lying unconscious on the deck. Everyone knew it was dangerous to move a seriously injured man, because he could have badly hurt his back, and the right thing would be to leave him where he lay until a doctor or medics could get to him, but there was no hope of help out here and no knowing how long it would be before the next wave would swamp the deck. It could happen at any time, and there was nothing for it but to pick the man up and carry him the shortest possible distance to the cabin under the whaleback, get the wet clothes off him and warm him up with dry covers and blankets. Then he mumbled something, so they knew that he wasn't dead.

Those who'd been up on the whaleback were ordered aft; they were soaked to the skin from the ice-cold sea. In the mess, Lárus was helped out of his oilskin smock; he was clearly in shock, shivering uncontrollably, but still protesting that he was fine. The bosun struggled to take off the deck glove from the hand that had gripped Lárus' collar; eventually he had to give up and ask for help, something he generally tried to avoid. But, try as he might, he couldn't get the glove off his hand, which was clenched so tight that the glove had to be cut off it. A thread of blood seeped out from under each of his nails, making this powerful hand look like the claw of a bird of prey.

"Hell, but the lad was a bit of a weight," he said, staring at his hand in wonder.

The second mate, lying uncomfortably and in pain under the whaleback, was still there. Some of the crew tried to check on him. It was plain that it would be too dangerous to try to bring him aft, to where the rest of the men were. But when they examined him they saw that he could move his hands and feet, as well as his fingers and toes. He was relieved, as he knew well what not being able to do this would have meant. But he was in terrible pain and coughing up blood. The skipper told the radio operator that it was worth getting the word out that they were in trouble, with a severely injured man on board on top of everything else, and instructed him to broadcast that they were in difficulties, with heavy weather and ice building up, and to get advice on how to treat the second mate's injuries. The radio operator went to work and sat in front of his equipment for a long time, rapidly transmitting in both plain speech and Morse. To begin with, he broadcast a general alert: "In serious difficulties, both lifeboats lost, clearing ice accretion but unable to keep up, ship listing, one badly injured man on board." Once it was sent, the radio operator tried to reach the company back in Iceland.

After a while he returned and said that Reykjavík had responded with the advice to treat the injured man with morphine, which should be in the ship's medical chest. He reported that he'd been able to make contact with a couple of trawlers from Iceland fishing over here in the western waters of the Atlantic. *Eyfirðingur* had also suffered heavy icing, but was some way to the south in warmer waters, where there was less danger of ice accretion, in addition to which *Eyfirðingur* ran on a steam engine rather than a diesel one, so they'd been able to use hot water from the boilers to melt the ice. *Garpur* was a long way from *Mávur*; *Poseidon* had just arrived on the grounds, but had hardly any fish on board, so it rode higher in the water and fewer waves were breaking over them. *Poseidon* would try to get a bearing on *Mávur* and might be able to reach them.

They opened the medicine chest, but there was no morphine in it; nobody knew who had taken it, or when. But there was brandy and some painkillers in the skipper's locker, and the first mate took them forward to try to cheer up his colleague lying there in pain.

———

It goes without saying that everyone hoped the weather would ease. According to all the usual laws of nature, it would. Every storm comes to an end, as the saying goes, and by now it was Sunday night and this one had lasted since midday the previous day. Everyone was exhausted. The communications equipment stopped working, and it was discovered that one of the aerials on the wheelhouse roof had come down under the weight of the ice, and the other one was halfway down. The radio operator wrapped himself up warm and clambered onto the wheelhouse roof, with three deckhands holding on to him. First they cleared the ice from the radar scanner until it began to turn again, and then the radio operator managed to fix the aerials and they climbed back down; they could use the radio now, to get the weather forecast for the Newfoundland waters, including the Kittiwake Bank, but there was no change expected for the next twenty-four hours; just the same furious north-westerly gale.

It was possible to interpret the forecast as saying that the wind wouldn't be quite so harsh, not as bitter as it had been, but it sounded like the frost would be even worse, rather than better, with an air temperature of minus fourteen to minus eighteen.

The skipper mulled things over. Everyone on board was worn out – the men in the engine room, the galley, and for that matter, those up in the wheelhouse – but the ones who had taken the brunt of it all were the deck crew. There had been no rest after that spell of heavy fishing, as they'd been out in the frost cracking ice ever since. They'd hardly had a chance to take off their oilskins. But they kept going, as the wind and the sea spray continued to pelt the deck, the wheelhouse and not least the whaleback which the four men had managed to clear surprisingly well. But it would ice over again, and in fact was well on the way to doing just that, and it would be a colder-hearted man than this skipper who would send his men out again into such danger. One lay forward, badly injured and in pain and all alone, another had been saved by a miracle, and a third had a badly injured hand after saving the second man's life. If this was to continue for at least another twenty-four hours, then their only hope might well be to turn and run before the weather, to try and reach the warmer seas where the *Eyfirðingur* was; it would be a ten- or twelve-hour steam, maybe as little as eight, if everything went well.

But bringing the ship about needed preparation. Men were sent aft to the boat deck and the casing, to break up as much as they could of the ice there while they were still sheltered by the ship's being head to wind. The skipper thought that maybe the ship wouldn't be as awkward in a following sea, perhaps not as sloppy, now that the heavy lifeboats were gone. The engine room crew had to be alerted and told to be ready to respond; they might have to slow down rapidly, or even go astern. Everything aft was carefully sealed. The first mate himself took the wheel. They ramped up the engine power and the ship began to come about, turning to starboard. Those watching the waves saw the manoeuvre, the others could feel it; the mate peered at the compass card, watching the lubber line pass 360 degrees – zero – due north – and began to count as it passed East, until it pointed to between 110 and 120 degrees, when a heavy wave rolled over the ship's port quarter. The ship almost lay over all the way on its side. Every man on board grabbed for the nearest handhold. Water lapped at the wheelhouse's starboard windows and gushed, ice-cold, through the window the skipper had been standing at since the previous morning, spraying in around the frame of the wooden door leading out to the wing.

At the same instant the mate lost all control over the ship's movement, and it carried on turning with the storm behind it, now heading due south, and nobody on board was in any doubt that their final moments were at hand. Only the foremast and the portside gallows emerged from the seething mass of angry water.

The second mate, lying alone and unable to move in the cabin forward under the whaleback, was thrown from his bunk onto the floor, where he lay fully awake; the pain in his back and insides sharpened his consciousness, and he heard everything that was happening around him. He was a good swimmer, and he knew how sound changes when you plunge below the surface. The second mate saw his life pass before his eyes – it really did happen, then – and then saw his wife and children. He decided to recite every prayer he could remember and the Gospel on his journey into eternity, and maybe his family at home in Kópavogur would somehow hear or sense it.

It was the evening of Sunday, the eighth of February.

The radio operator thought that his last action ought to be to send a distress call, even if it was only to let the outside world know that they had gone. But he'd been thrown across the floor and was unable to reach his equipment, and in any case, the impact had put the radio out of action again.

Down in the engine room, they tried to hang on to anything they could grab hold of, and if the roar of the engine hadn't smothered all sound their terrified screams would have been heard. The chief and the third engineer had both roped themselves into their positions, so that they would be able to respond to the telegraph. In the wheelhouse above, at the open window through which the water continued to flood whenever waves came over them, the skipper saw that the bow was buried deep in the wall of water rising in front of them. They were heading down. He snatched at the telegraph and rang full astern, on full power, using even the extra margin of power to be used only in emergencies. Full power meant 84 revolutions of the shaft, and now he ordered 105. *Something* had to be tried. At the same time, he yelled the same instruction down the copper speaking tube. It was a relief that the engine was still running, and he hoped the burst of emergency power wouldn't overload it.

Down below there was an inclinometer which had become jammed, its needle pointing to sixty degrees. Everyone knew that whether they lived or died depended on the ship's next movement. Which way would it go? A second later, they heard and felt the propeller running the other way, astern. As soon as the skipper judged that this had hauled them clear and they were no longer heading for the bottom of the sea, he rang down for full speed ahead, again telling them to use the emergency power, and then the bow dragged itself over to port, slowly at first, a little at a time, until they were once more heading into the weather and the wind. They slowed the engine; they were still alive, still on the surface.

Everyone knew that this wasn't over, that the sword of Damocles still hung over them. Ships had foundered all around them, and there was every likelihood that *Mávur* would be the next to go. Earlier that evening there had been a report from that great ship, the *Queen Elizabeth*, which was steaming westwards not far to the south, that they had reckoned an eighteen-metre wave height and one of the storm's bursts of fury had knocked out a couple of that high-sided ship's bridge windows. Even though everyone on board *Mávur* was exhausted, there was nothing for it but to push on through what seemed to be a losing battle with the weather.

Down in the galley the cooks did their best to maintain a steady flow of hot food. The head cook had decided to make meat soup that evening, which everyone knows is food that gives you energy, made with mutton cooked in a broth of swedes, carrots, herbs and rice, but when the boat heeled hard over on its side as they tried to come about, most of it parted company with the pot and landed on the floor. The meat and the swedes were saved and served up steaming hot in the mess; the crew could pick up a chunk of meat with a knife or fork to gnaw it, or they could just use their fingers. There's energy to be had in this kind of fare, not least in the fattiest pieces.

They pulled on their warmest padded coats – most of them using the sheepskin padding from green V.I.R. overcoats under their smock tops – and then it was back out into the cold, the dark and foul weather, to hammer more ice off the ship, which was again perceptibly gaining weight, righting itself only sluggishly after each roll. Was this ever going to end? They knew that, with the ship so badly off-kilter, it would take only a few extra kilos for the keel to face upwards instead of down.

They still had their two hours' rest in every twenty-four, and some of those who came in from the deck were dead to the world as soon as they sat down, sometimes with a half-chewed mouthful of food, asleep or unconscious, not even waking up when their heads rolled against a deckhead or a table, before they were woken up with a shake and made to understand that the ice wasn't going to take a break while the crew was sleeping. Some of the men vanished and were found later, huddled in a bunk, dazed and sobbing, and ordered back to work. One deckhand had sat in the mess for a long time, rambling incoherently about legendary ghost cats and merpeople, chain-smoking and drinking coffee for two hours or more.

"He's off his head," someone said.

Once it was clear that he wouldn't be persuaded out onto the deck again, they decided the best thing to do with him was to bundle him up to the wheelhouse and put him on a steering watch, which released the man who was at the wheel. But these measures proved useless, or worse, since the new man at the wheel didn't hear the instructions, but simply continued to mutter about ghoul cats as he stared with dead eyes into the distance. They saw that he had wet himself, and he clung so tightly to the wheel that, when the others in the wheelhouse went to adjust its position, this man who was holding on to it with all that strength made it even more difficult to steer. Finally his hands were peeled off the wheel, one finger at a time, and he was left to lie on the floor for a while.

Young Lárus managed to doze for a few minutes, shivering himself to sleep, and instinctively woke up when the ship began to turn and lay over hard, almost all the way over on one side, and when he felt that he'd managed to pull himself together he wordlessly tried to find dry clothes. He found a smock top, which was tight, wet and slippery inside, and for a moment Lárus couldn't find the sleeves and was caught in this large but restrictive thing, unable to move in the smelly, stuffy darkness.

This is what it must be like to drown, was the thought that flashed into his mind; he found his way around the smock, his hands forced themselves into the sleeves and his head popped up from the depths, past the neckline, and he gasped for air as his heart hammered in his chest. Then he reached for damp deck gloves and a tool, and it was back out onto the deck to break more ice. Although the lifeboats were gone, the davits were still there, two each side, collecting a great deal of ice.

Two of the men spent most of the night hammering ice from these frames, struggling to keep up. Others were at work getting rid of everything that could be let go, throwing wires, nets, baskets and tubs, aerials and fishing gear over the side, anything on which the ice could collect. The bosun had wrapped sticking plasters over his fingernails so that the blood no longer seeped out from under them, and then he bound his fingers in more plasters to lessen the pain. When the ship had rolled hard over onto its side, he'd held on with all his strength and been consumed with fear, and as it righted itself he felt a strange wonder at this sudden feeling he had of having to fight against this death staring him in the face. He thought to himself that, since he'd managed to save young Lárus' life, it would be a shame if they were to be lost now, which would render what he had done worthless, and there was something good about having survived what had happened to them up on the whaleback, in spite of the injuries and everything. Then he was called up to the wheelhouse and asked if he could take the wheel with his injured hand. A man was needed to replace the one who'd been frozen by fear, and the bosun said that he could easily do it, that there wasn't much wrong with him, that he could also hold a hammer and crack ice. He said that his fist was shaped perfectly to hold an axe handle, and showed the skipper his bound-up hand. The radio operator, the man who had read all the books and who knew so much, was there, and the bosun asked him what the truth of it was; had Leifur Eiríksson been nicknamed Leifur the Lucky because he had found America, or Vinland as they had called it? Always generous with his knowledge, the Sparks replied that no, it wasn't like that, Leifur had earned his nickname by rescuing men from a certain shipwreck. In fact, it hadn't been that far away, just south-west of Greenland, if he remembered rightly. Being able to save a life had been a sign of good fortune, or luck. The bosun nodded. He was sure that's what he'd heard too.

The radio operator was done up smartly, with a tie around his neck, and said that if he was going to be on his way to meet his maker he wanted to look respectable. The skipper didn't smile at this; his face hardened. He wasn't going to give any hint that the game might be lost, and didn't appreciate it when others talked that way. Both the head cook and the second cook had carried stacked trays of piping hot food into the mess, telling anyone who would listen that if we're going to die it didn't make it any better to do it on an empty stomach.

As day broke on Monday morning, the frost was no less bitter than it had been, but the wind appeared to have eased. Or so it seemed to the crew, but it turned out to be a false hope, and before long the weather had whipped itself up once more, the sea swelled and the ship was again heavy and sluggish in the waves. They lost more and more of the crew, as their spirits broke and they became unable to work, started talking to themselves, and were told to lie down and go to sleep, which they sadly didn't do.

They'd been labouring in the galley overnight, roasting all the smoked pork left on board, and a mountain of sliced meat was on the messroom table along with bottles of cold milk – and of course coffee – and they had also taken joints of salted meat from the barrels and roasted those in the ovens. It was better that way, because the ship's movements ruled out boiling anything in a big pot, and roasting did the job just as well.

The younger one of the two engine room greasers was out of action, and the chief engineer went up to the wheelhouse to confer with the skipper. The lifeboat frames, the davits, were a real problem. They were made of steel and weighed a couple of tonnes each, a weight easily doubled by the ice that had collected on them. The chief's thinking was that maybe they could be burned through, and there was no shortage of oxy-acetylene on board to do the job. It was obvious that this would be a tough and hazardous undertaking, but as things stood everything they had to do on board was arduous and dangerous. The bosun was back in the wheelhouse. After his last turn at the wheel he had gone out on deck with a sledge-hammer to smash ice, but his hand turned out to be so weak that he could hardly grip the handle and it had rattled around in his fist. So now he was working with the chief to manhandle bottles of gas out onto the wheelhouse wing. The chief connected the hoses, and the bosun tied a rope around his waist and fixed himself to the rail, then stood in the lee of the door keeping an eye out for breaking waves around them, and holding on to the rope tied around the chief's waist, just in case. They had broken the ice off the after davit on the starboard side. Every now and again the ship lay over, like icebergs and vast ice floes do when they gain weight on top or melt below, and overbalance and turn right over. The young chief engineer began to cut, without mask or goggles, stretched out on the smooth ice. It felt to him like cutting frozen meat with a blunt knife, but he made progress all the same.

Sometimes the skipper noticed that he was extremely sore; his knees and hips hurt, and he was getting stomach pains and headaches. He had found that tobacco was the most effective remedy, both cigarettes and snuff, and he needed a constant supply of coffee to keep his head as clear as possible. There was no getting away from it; he had no choice but to stand there by the telegraph and the open window until this was all over. He only took breaks to quickly go to the toilet, and would immediately be back in his place, gazing out into the storm, watching the waves that rolled past, as high as mountains.

A big ship passed them once, slowly and surely, and they

saw that it was a Russian factory ship, one of those that took catches of redfish from the Russian trawlers working these grounds, reducing them to fishmeal and fish oil. The skipper asked the radio operator if it was worth trying to contact the Russians, but he couldn't get through to them. He didn't know their call sign and there was no guarantee that they understood the English with which he tried to call them. Besides, they didn't know exactly what they could say to the Russians, and there was no obvious way for them to help *Mávur*'s crew. But the men in the wheelhouse thought that the Russians must have seen them, that someone on board there must have noticed this ice-covered Icelandic trawler lying half-swamped under the weight of the storm. But then the Russian disappeared into the darkness, leaving *Mávur* and its crew alone again.

They knew that their survival hung in the balance, and depended on whether or not the davits could be cut away, and apart from a few short breaks the chief had been at work on the first one now for more than an hour. The bosun, standing under the shelter aft as he watched the sea around them, sometimes called him in, and then the chief would hurry across, cutting torch in hand, and they would wait while another wave crashed over the deck. Eventually the chief almost finished with the first of the davits, and now it was only a question of time before this two-tonne lump of iron gave up under its own weight; and then it would depend on which way the ship was rolling, whether it would drop overboard and into the sea, or inwards, onto the deck, which would leave them worse off than before.

The bosun and one of the hands picked up planks and a knocking-out pin, and tried to find footholds on the icy deck; as the ship rolled, the chief cut the last of the supports while the others strained and pushed, and the davit gave way. The lifeboat frame aft on the starboard side rolled into the seething water and disappeared down to the bottom, to join the redfish.

A rest would have been welcome before the next effort, but there was no time. The chief engineer had a wife and newborn twins back home in Reykjavík; a pair of Christmas babies whom he had no intention of leaving, so they carried the gas bottles over to the other side and started afresh, working on the aft frame on the port side, and for the next two hours the bosun stood there in the lee of the wheelhouse door, watching the chief and the blue glow from his torch. They kept cutting, between having to run for shelter, and then there was only one more to go.

This continued all that Monday morning; all those still on their feet were battering ice off the ship, hammering and chopping, even though their hands and whole bodies were sore, while the skipper stood at the wheelhouse window and watched for breakers, yelling a warning to hold on or run for shelter if necessary. Lárus was at the wheel, feeling like he could neither sleep nor stay awake. He was in a condition that allowed him to stand upright, be aware of his surroundings and use his hands, but the world around him had become something unreal, a dreamland, with voices and sounds blending with strange echoes and a grinding in his ears. On the way to take his turn at the wheel, he had taken a quick look in the chart room and seen the chart lying there, the one covering the seas bordering Newfoundland, and all of a sudden he felt that he was looking at a very different chart, the one of the area where the *Titanic* was reckoned to have foundered, the one in the Danish or Norwegian book that his father had. Or rather, it was the same chart, of the same sea and with the same land to the west, Newfoundland, Nova Scotia and Labrador, and it was as if he was in a different world while he stood at the wheel, no longer sure on which ship he was sailing, and with the feeling that any moment now he would be on the way to the seabed where the wreck of that famous liner lay, where he would get to see it. Maybe he'd be the first man to take a look at it, before the cold sea had a chance to snuff him out. But he kept the ship heading into the wind – impeccably, the skipper thought – and that was important.

In the cabin under the whaleback forward, the injured second mate lay in the lower bunk, and for company he had a deckhand who'd been put in the next bunk, a man who was mentally and physically incapable of working, who had been stretched out on one of the messroom benches, trembling and holding a disjointed conversation with himself. The men had decided that, if he had to lie somewhere, they might be able to make the second mate's life more bearable by giving him some company.

"Keep an eye open for anything you can do to help him," they said to the deckhand as they took him forward. "He's not supposed to move at all."

But the deeply troubled new arrival was little consolation for the suffering mate. That Monday the bow dug itself deep into a wave twice, taking them beneath the surface as the whole ship headed downwards. The sounds there in the crew quarters forward were very different when they were surrounded by air rather than water, and every time it happened a long and piercing wail came from the deckhand, not loud but very clear, so long that it sounded inhuman. Once the engine had been put full astern, with all the din that went with it, and they had managed to haul themselves back up, the bow pitched into the waves again; the man would sigh nervously and make no reply to anything said to him.

The second aft davit disappeared into the ocean, and the skipper immediately noticed that the ship's stability had improved. Although the chief engineer had spent the last four hours out in the cold and the weather with a cutting torch, there was still no opportunity for him to take a rest. Two more davits were still attached, the forward pair, heavy weights that continued to collect ice. The chief and the bosun agreed that it would be best to be rid of them all while it was still daylight, that it would be better not to be doing this as Monday evening brought darkness with it. The skipper was also apprehensive about the night ahead, but hoped that it would mean the last of this terrible weather. Going by the forecast, it would calm down and become warmer in the course of Tuesday, but until then they would somehow have to keep themselves afloat, and the right way up.

The radio operator emerged from behind his equipment, his tie still knotted at his throat. The skipper shot him a glance and it crossed his mind to suggest that he should shave and smarten himself up, especially if he intended to be in keeping with the silk tie, but he said nothing. The radio operator told him that he had been in contact with the *Poseidon*, which had fixed a bearing on them and was not far off. They were making slow progress but would be alongside by evening.

Then they heard that the third davit had also gone. A genius, this young chief engineer, they said, a genius and a hero.

Heavy ice had again collected on the whaleback, and now there was as much as before, and the boat was heavy by the bow, but the skipper would avoid sending men forward for as long as he could. He had done it once already, and it was a miracle that he hadn't sent those two men to their deaths. The glacier of ice that had formed over the winches in front of the superstructure was again close to reaching up to the wheelhouse windows, and even though there were men at work with hammers, the ice was so thick that they made little impression on it. They had shackled the winch drums down when they'd made ready to steam home after the fishroom had been filled, so they couldn't run the winches to break the ice off them, but the skipper thought that they ought to give it a try anyway. They probably wouldn't have to move the drums more than half an inch or so to crack the ice. He suggested it to the mate, who agreed, and went down to the engine room to talk to the second and third engineers; both were red-eyed and hoarse, but said they could quickly clutch in the winches.

"At worst, nothing'll happen," the third engineer said.

The mate took three of the able-bodied deckhands with him out onto the deck to watch what would happen, to see if things began to move and be ready to react. The skipper peered into the waves and called first into the copper speaking tube and then out onto the deck.

"Try it now!"

There was a grinding of machinery, and they recognised the sound of the winches – different though it was, loud but somehow smothered; they heard the sound of the ice cracking, and then it broke into pieces. Down in the engine room the winches were stopped. Large slabs broke off the drums, practically miniature ice floes that dropped to the deck on either side and lodged themselves against the gunwales. Now the race was on to smash these into smaller pieces so that they would wash out through the scuppers, which was a dance with death, as the ice chunks skidded across to the middle of the deck when the ship righted itself, and the men with the hammers had to chase them. Before they could be split into smaller pieces, a breaker rose up and the skipper called down a warning to the men to take shelter, which they managed without any injuries.

The upper end of the ice mountain was still left, hanging in mid-air above the winches on the superstructure. It was no easy task to hack at it from below, and extremely hazardous, because there was every chance that a broken-off chunk of ice could drop, heavily and hard, onto the man below it. The upshot was that two of the deckhands let themselves be suspended on ropes from the wheelhouse roof and battered the ice from above; they managed to clear most of it, and then the crew smashed it into smaller pieces on the deck as the storm continued to pound them.

Darkness began to fall. One more night of heavy weather was ahead. The chief had managed to cut away the last of the davits and it had fallen into the sea. He had hardly flinched for a moment the whole time, but now he sat in the mess, chilled to the bone and swaddled in every warm blanket that could be found, twitching and shivering so hard that he couldn't eat what was given to him. He had spent more than seven hours on the frozen deck, unable to see anything, the world having become a single blue flash that burned and scorched everything in its path.

They saw the lights of another ship: the trawler *Poseidon* had arrived. The crew gazed at it as if it was a miracle, as if they had seen God's hand at work, and maybe this was how it was when the disciples saw their redeemer come walking across the water to them. They were no longer alone in the world, among furious seas and howling winds. The lights came and went, even though the ships were close to each other, as the darkness and the squalls obscured their view and the two ships dipped in turn into the deep troughs. The two radio operators talked to each other, and *Poseidon* reported that they were in good shape, riding high in the water and no large seas breaking over them, and the crew were able to keep pace with the ice, knocking it off as it formed. They had heard nothing from the *Harpa*, except for what they thought might have been the beginning of a Mayday call – but after that there was nothing else from the thirty men who'd been on board.

Poseidon would stay at *Mávur*'s side until the weather eased; it had been three days and nights of bitter frost accompanied by heavy seas, but this couldn't go on for ever. Then they would seek out warmer waters and, God willing, be able to set course for home. Everyone could see that it would be touch and go as to whether *Mávur* would remain afloat that long. There were discussions about how they could get from one ship to the other, whether *Mávur*'s crew could be pulled over to *Poseidon* in a breeches-buoy, but that idea was rejected. In this kind of weather, and rolling hard, it would be impossible. Lárus stood alone at the wheel, relieved like the others, knowing that there was another ship close by. But he couldn't avoid the thought, the question that was on his mind, of how on earth those on the other ship could be of any assistance to *Mávur*'s crew.

If the ship were to sink suddenly, after capsizing, what could they do? Some would be trapped inside the sinking ship, and those on deck would be pitched into the ice-cold sea in the black night and screaming gale. What could they do? Even with another steel ship pitching through the waves a hundred or so metres away?

Nobody can survive more than a minute or two in water so cold that it's below freezing. And *Mávur* no longer had any lifeboats, apart from a couple of rubber rafts in boxes, waiting to be inflated, one forward and one aft. The skipper had ordered the men to make sure that the ice was regularly cleared from those boxes. But how would they be rescued?

Poseidon asked if they could be ready with an inflated life raft on the deck, which *Mávur*'s crew could get into if they felt that the boat was on the way down, but everyone could see that it was impossible. They wouldn't be able to handle a rubber life raft in this kind of wind and these seas. So Lárus did his best to brush aside such thoughts, telling himself that he was giving himself waking nightmares, which wasn't surprising considering he had hardly slept more than a few moments for days on end. Since they hadn't sunk so far, there was no reason to be certain that they would, despite the fact that the ship never managed to right itself properly after being hurled to one side or the other. There were still men outside in the storm breaking ice off the superstructure, and the echoes of their blows carried into the wheelhouse.

But the same thought returned. What if they were to roll over now? Lárus imagined, or decided to imagine, that he would rush out through the door at the side of the wheelhouse that remained uppermost, running for it before the floor became a vertical wall. He'd be able to walk across the ship's side and onto the keel as it appeared; the green-painted keel that he had seen when *Mávur* had been hauled up onto the slipway to be painted. They would be watching from the *Poseidon*, and somehow they would be able to pluck to safety those who had made it to the keel of the sinking *Mávur*. But maybe they wouldn't sink, and they had said that the morning would bring fairer weather.

———

The morning was fairer.

As the day passed, it was finally possible to risk bringing the ship about before the weather, and they did. That day, they saw kittiwakes flying over the sea for the first time since Friday. These are storm birds, and when they appear you're among friends. *Mávur* and the *Poseidon* slowly steamed towards warmer seas. Many of the crew had suffered frostbite, most of them were wracked with aches; the oldest deckhand hadn't shut his eyes since the weather had closed in, and on the steam home he had such heart palpitations that the others were afraid he wouldn't survive, while he felt that, although he couldn't do anything else, he couldn't be a seaman any longer either. He had a wife ashore who always seemed to him unhappy, and they had stopped talking long ago. They had a son in his twenties who had never achieved anything, had dropped out of school, couldn't hold down a job and wanted nothing more than to hang around with his buddies listening to Elvis Presley.

There wasn't much talk on board, on the steam home. It

was as if nobody had anything to talk about any longer, or maybe there was nothing that came to mind other than the wild weather of the previous days, and nobody wanted to talk about that. The men were drained. Not much work was done, just the most necessary tasks in the galley and the engine room. The skipper and the first mate took the wheelhouse watches in turn, with another man at the wheel, and there was a sofa in the back where they could take a nap.

There were lumps in many throats as the city lights drew near. As he saw the leading lights, Lárus fought back his tears and managed to swallow them.

———

It was the middle of the night when *Mávur* RE-335 docked in Reykjavík, half-past two on a pitch-black morning, but all the same the harbour was thronged with people. There was a long, white ambulance with red crosses on the side, to take the injured second mate away. An aircraft had come to meet them as they approached the west coast, just to see them, to make absolutely sure that the ship was still afloat on the surface, and the good news had been broadcast on the radio; joyful news, following the other news about *Harpa*: the people waiting for the crew on the dock were subdued, because *Harpa* had finally been written off earlier that day, and the search abandoned.

Mávur's crew made their way off the ship one by one. Some were embraced, people talked in low voices, and there were tears. The oldest deckhand was met by his wife and son who had come in the family's old rattletrap, and the wife threw her arms around him while the son opened the driver's door for his father and then sat in the back, knees against the seat so that it wouldn't tip backwards, as it had been inclined to do ever since something underneath it had broken.

"This is good," the oldest deckhand thought.

Lárus' parents stood there with his little brother, and they were all somehow grey, but beautifully so. And this brought everything to a close.

———

I felt it was the right thing to do, to recall that time, as I'm the ship's namesake. Many of the crew cursed the skipper, out loud or under their breath, for driving us on, letting us have only two hours a day to rest, before they realised that in all that time he hadn't moved once from his post in the wheelhouse. For three and a half days he stood there, with nothing but coffee and tobacco to keep him going, and when he finally walked to his bunk he needed two men to hold him up so that he wouldn't pass out. He himself ordered them to do that.

There were thirty-two of us on board, all of us experienced

seamen or in the process of gaining experience. Only eight of us dared go to sea again after that, and the rest found themselves work ashore; those who were capable of working, that is. I started to prepare myself to write this almost right away, even though I wasn't able to do so until much later.

The two of us who shared a cabin in the worst place on board, forward where the anchor clanked against the side right next to our ears, and where nobody apart from the two of us who had found ourselves there wanted to be, started to chat occasionally on the trip home, just as if we were friends. He told me about the woman and the child who were the guiding lights of his life, the only purpose and meaning he had found in life. As we approached Reykjavík and the city's lights shone ahead of us, he had changed into his best, bootlace tie and all. There was only a little aftershave left in his two bottles for him to splash on; he put it in himself instead, shaking up the contents of the bottles into a froth, like a milkshake, one Portuguese and the other Aqua Velva, and drank it down quickly, grimacing as he did so, which made him just like other men who drink that way: plain crazy and as far removed as you can be from someone with a chance of winning over beautiful women or their children. We didn't see a lot of each other after we left the ship and he dropped dead in the street a few years later. The editor of *Morgunblaðið*'s cultural magazine, which had often published his verses, wrote him a beautiful obituary, calling him the Poet of Darkness.

————

More than two hundred lives were lost on the same grounds where we had spent that trip, half of them on the Kittiwake Bank, while we were fighting against the ice and death did its best to drag us down to the seabed. Now they are down there in the deep with the people who were lost with the *Titanic*, and they'll neither see nor be seen by anyone again. That's unless they're so fortunate as to be pulled up in the nets of one of the trawlers fishing those grounds. They'll come up full of the gas that bloats those who are retrieved from the weight of the deep sea above them, maybe with their stomachs puffed out and mouths open, like the redfish, and at night I see myself coming to the surface that way with the others, crowded into a trawl.

EINAR KÁRASON started his career writing poetry for literary magazines, and published his first novel in 1981. Before *Storm Birds* he was best known for his novel *Þar sem djöflaeyjan rís*, which was translated into English as *Devil's Island* (2000) and made into a film.

QUENTIN BATES is a writer and translator who has written a series of crime novels set in present-day Iceland.